"Y..."

"Have yo... ...abeth ranted on. "You're going to work in a *bar* for a living?" She said it as if she were talking about hanging out with cockroaches. "What about your parents? What about your future? You can't just drop out of school. I mean—"

"*First* of all," Todd interrupted harshly, causing Elizabeth's mouth to snap shut. "Where do you get off telling me how to live my life? It's not like it's mattered to you at all in the past, oh, I don't know, *year.*"

Elizabeth's eyes narrowed, and her whole face went pink, but Todd wasn't about to stop.

He was going to tell her off, big time.

Bantam Books in the Sweet Valley University series.
Ask your bookseller for the books you have missed.

#1 COLLEGE GIRLS	#28 ELIZABETH'S HEARTBREAK
#2 LOVE, LIES, AND JESSICA WAKEFIELD	#29 ONE LAST KISS
	#30 BEAUTY AND THE BEACH
#3 WHAT YOUR PARENTS DON'T KNOW . . .	#31 THE TRUTH ABOUT RYAN
	#32 THE BOYS OF SUMMER
#4 ANYTHING FOR LOVE	#33 OUT OF THE PICTURE
#5 A MARRIED WOMAN	#34 SPY GIRL
#6 THE LOVE OF HER LIFE	#35 UNDERCOVER ANGELS
#7 GOOD-BYE TO LOVE	#36 HAVE YOU HEARD ABOUT ELIZABETH?
#8 HOME FOR CHRISTMAS	
#9 SORORITY SCANDAL	#37 BREAKING AWAY
#10 NO MEANS NO	#38 GOOD-BYE, ELIZABETH
#11 TAKE BACK THE NIGHT	#39 ELIZABETH ♥ NEW YORK
#12 COLLEGE CRUISE	#40 PRIVATE JESSICA
#13 SS HEARTBREAK	#41 ESCAPE TO NEW YORK
#14 SHIPBOARD WEDDING	#42 SNEAKING IN
#15 BEHIND CLOSED DOORS	#43 THE PRICE OF LOVE
#16 THE OTHER WOMAN	#44 LOVE ME ALWAYS
#17 DEADLY ATTRACTION	#45 DON'T LET GO
#18 BILLIE'S SECRET	#46 I'LL NEVER LOVE AGAIN
#19 BROKEN PROMISES, SHATTERED DREAMS	#47 YOU'RE NOT MY SISTER
	#48 NO RULES
#20 HERE COMES THE BRIDE	#49 STRANDED
#21 FOR THE LOVE OF RYAN	#50 SUMMER OF LOVE
#22 ELIZABETH'S SUMMER LOVE	#51 LIVING TOGETHER
#23 SWEET KISS OF SUMMER	#52 FOOLING AROUND
#24 HIS SECRET PAST	#53 TRUTH OR DARE
#25 BUSTED!	#54 RUSH WEEK
#26 THE TRIAL OF JESSICA WAKEFIELD	#55 THE FIRST TIME
#27 ELIZABETH AND TODD FOREVER	#56 DROPPING OUT

And don't miss these Sweet Valley University Thriller Editions:

#1 WANTED FOR MURDER	#10 CHANNEL X
#2 HE'S WATCHING YOU	#11 LOVE AND MURDER
#3 KISS OF THE VAMPIRE	#12 DON'T ANSWER THE PHONE
#4 THE HOUSE OF DEATH	#13 CYBERSTALKER: THE RETURN OF WILLIAM WHITE, PART I
#5 RUNNING FOR HER LIFE	
#6 THE ROOMMATE	#14 DEADLY TERROR: THE RETURN OF WILLIAM WHITE, PART II
#7 WHAT WINSTON SAW	
#8 DEAD BEFORE DAWN	#15 LOVING THE ENEMY
#9 KILLER AT SEA	#16 KILLER PARTY

Visit the Official Sweet Valley Web Site on the Internet at:

http://www.sweetvalley.com

SWEET VALLEY UNIVERSITY®

Dropping Out

Written by
Laurie John

Created by
FRANCINE PASCAL

BANTAM BOOKS
NEW YORK · TORONTO · LONDON · SYDNEY · AUCKLAND

RL: 8, AGES 014 AND UP

DROPPING OUT
A Bantam Book / March 2000

Sweet Valley High® and Sweet Valley University®
are registered trademarks of Francine Pascal.
Conceived by Francine Pascal.

Copyright © 2000 by Francine Pascal.
Cover art copyright © 2000 by 17th Street Productions, Inc.

All rights reserved. No part of this book may be reproduced or transmitted
in any form or by any means, electronic or mechanical,
including photocopying, recording, or by any information
storage and retrieval system, without permission in
writing from the publisher.
For information address: Bantam Books.

Produced by 17th Street Productions, Inc.
33 West 17th Street
New York, NY 10011.

If you purchased this book without a cover you should be aware
that this book is stolen property. It was reported as "unsold and
destroyed" to the publisher and neither the author nor the publisher has received any payment for this "stripped book."

ISBN: 0-553-49308-6

Visit us on the Web! www.randomhouse.com/teens

Published simultaneously in the United States and Canada

Bantam Books is an imprint of Random House Children's Books, a
division of Random House, Inc. BANTAM BOOKS and the rooster
colophon are registered trademarks of Random House, Inc. Bantam Books,
1540 Broadway, New York, New York 10036.

PRINTED IN THE UNITED STATES OF AMERICA

OPM   0 9 8 7 6 5 4 3 2 1

To Richard Wenk

Chapter
One

_____

"Hey, mister! Your zipper's down!"

Todd Wilkins blushed and stared at the very helpful, yet far too loud four-year-old boy pointing up at him.

"Thanks for the tip, kid," he muttered, zipping his fly as he continued on his mad dash for his car. He couldn't bring himself to meet the eyes of the kid's mother, but he was sure she was laughing at him.

I probably look like a lunatic, Todd thought as he scrambled down the concrete steps outside his apartment building and tried to remember where he'd parked the Beemer at four o'clock that morning. After a long night cleaning up after partyers and flat-out drunks at Frankie's, Todd had crashed hard. And of course, he'd slept through his alarm—*again.* Now he was beyond late for class, he smelled like a brewery, and he had more facial hair than he'd ever thought was acceptable.

Todd finally spotted his car about half a block down the street, illegally parked in front of a fire hydrant. How had he missed that last night? Luckily there was no ticket.

"Thank God for small favors," Todd said, repeating one of his mother's favorite one-liners. He attempted to tuck in his shirt with one hand as he reached for the door handle with the other, but he just ended up getting all bunched and twisted. He pulled the shirt out completely and unlocked the car. As soon as he was safely inside, he gripped the steering wheel and took a deep breath.

"Okay, calm yourself," he muttered, running a hand over his shaggy, dirty brown hair. Todd glanced at his haggard reflection in the mirror and winced. Then he glanced at the clock and winced again. He started the car and peeled out into the street.

"It's not that bad," Todd told himself as he flipped the radio on to his favorite station. If he lucked out and didn't hit any traffic, he might even have time to grab a muffin or something at Yum-Yum's before his class.

Todd turned the car onto Route 18 and started to sing along with the music in an attempt to further calm his nerves. His whole body was aching for more sleep, but his brain was on hyperdrive.

Last night the bar had been packed, and Todd had been on top of his game. He'd kept everything ready for Cathy, the bartender, broken up two fights, smashed only one glass, and helped the manager, Rita, when she was panicking over a discrepancy in the books. Todd had easily found the mistake—a botched entry in last week's petty-cash column. Rita had been so prolific with her thanks, Todd had felt like he'd just solved the world's hunger problem.

A smile twitched at the corners of Todd's mouth as he came to a stop at a red light. It had been a long time since he'd felt like he was actually being useful to anyone. It wasn't a half-bad feeling. It almost made up for his dread over the fact that he hadn't cracked open his marketing book since the last class.

The light turned green, and Todd hit the gas. The car made a loud sputtering noise, and then everything went silent. Everything except for the car horns that immediately started blaring behind him. A line of sweat popped up on his forehead as he glanced in the rearview mirror. The ruddy, hairy guy in the truck behind him was yelling his head off.

Todd tried turning the key in the ignition, but all it did was make a faint clicking noise. Every single light on his dashboard was lit up—from the *E* on his gas gauge to the check-engine light.

"Why now?" Todd blurted out, slamming the wheel with the heel of his hand. He knew he had a full gas tank—he wasn't that stupid. So what the hell was causing the problem?

Todd flipped on his hazard lights and got out of the car.

"What the hell are you doing!" the truck driver screamed, leaning out his window. "Get moving, boy!"

"Go around!" Todd shouted back. "The thing's dead."

Truck-driver guy rolled his eyes and swore under his breath. "Damn privileged kids and their damn foreign cars."

Todd had to clench his fists to keep from exploding as he walked around to the hood of his car. *Just ignore him*, he thought. *It's not worth it*. Checking his watch, Todd realized a muffin was out of the question. His stomach grumbled loudly as he popped the hood. A blast of steam billowed out, and the air reeked of burned rubber. Todd waved his hand in front of his nose.

Forget the muffin. It looked like marketing class was out of the question too.

"Tell your daddy to buy American next time, kid!" the trucker yelled as he swerved around Todd's dying Beemer and ran the now yellow light.

It was all Todd could do to keep from screaming a string of curses in the guy's wake. What was

4

wrong with everybody these days? People just assumed he was overprivileged because he was young and he had a BMW.

Okay, so Todd's family did have a lot of money, but that didn't mean Todd used it—not even for upkeep on his car. That was why the Beemer was blasting its insides all over the street right now.

Todd rested his arms on the roof of his car and laid his head on his forearms. He took a deep breath, then looked up and down the street, hoping for a miracle in the form of a tow truck. His mouth twisted into a wry smile. What he wouldn't give for his overprivileged father to have given him a cell phone along with the car. There was a gas station down the road. Hopefully they had a tow truck. At the very least, they had to have a pay phone.

Todd reached into the car and grabbed his keys and his backpack. He hoisted his bag onto both shoulders, locked the car, and started walking.

Being a working man sucked.

Or was it being a college student that sucked?

Sam Burgess rolled over onto his chest and buried his face deep between his two plush feather pillows. He smiled in his slightly awake state and let out a contented sigh. This felt very, very good—this space between dreams and the comfort of his flannel sheets—the morning sunlight warming his bed. He could stay here forever.

Why am I so damned happy right now? Sam thought, blinking open his eyes and flipping onto his back. *It's Monday. I have three classes. And I woke up before my alarm went off.*

One glance at the digital alarm clock on his bedside table informed him that he could sleep for another hour, but he was fully awake and smiling. Sam. A guy who valued sleep more than girls valued their hair dryers.

A door slammed right behind his head, causing his paper-thin bedroom wall to shudder. Sam's eyes opened fully for the first time. Jessica had some nerve—

Suddenly a sweet, slightly off-key humming came floating through the wall, and Sam's heart started to pound. That wasn't Jessica. He'd know that inept singing voice anywhere. It was Elizabeth.

Elizabeth Wakefield.

And she was the reason he was smiling.

With a start, Sam raised himself up onto his elbows. The dream Sam had been having just before he woke up came rushing back to him. Elizabeth in his arms. In his bed. Curled up with her back against his chest. His face in her apple-scented hair. She'd been whispering to him. What was she whispering?

Sam started to sweat just thinking about it. He let out a quick burst of breath and rubbed his hands over his eyes, trying at once to clear the memory and clinging to it in an attempt to

6

remember what Elizabeth had said in his dream.

In the kitchen Elizabeth's humming grew louder. Sam imagined her in there, making a pot of coffee, pushing a strand of her blond hair out of her eyes, licking a crumb of toast off her lips.

"What's wrong with me?" Sam asked his room, pressing the heels of his hands against his temples. He flopped back onto his rumpled plaid sheets and groaned. Why had he let himself get close to Elizabeth this weekend? Why had he felt the need to swoop in and rescue her when that idiot med student had dumped her?

It was her problem. Her mistake. He should have just let her deal with the consequences. But no. He had to get sucked in. He had to sit there and hold her and comfort her for hours. He had to let himself feel her softness, hear her vulnerability.

He had to let himself fall.

"No," Sam said to himself, fully aware that he was acting like a lunatic. He pulled himself out of bed and walked over to his dresser mirror. He looked directly into his hazel eyes—still bleary with sleep—and set his jaw.

"You are not falling for her, Burgess," he said. "You can't let a little humming and a little girlie weepiness and some stupid apple-scented shampoo get to you." He took a deep breath, pulling in his stomach and puffing out his chest slightly. Then he let the breath out slowly. "You're fine."

He went back to his bed and plopped in, ready to force himself to get his extra hour of quality snooze time. The moment he hit the sheets, Elizabeth started singing.

"But I don't know how to let you go," she sang in her not-quite-on-the-note voice. *"No, I don't know how to let you go."*

Sam felt a slow smile creep across his face and snorted a laugh. She was so cute. She was probably using the butter knife as a microphone. He just—

Ugh!

Sam pulled the covers over his head and squeezed his eyes shut, as if that could possibly block out her voice.

"Don't let go, Sam. Just don't let go."

Suddenly Sam was back in the dream. That was what Elizabeth had been whispering. His insides turned to mush as he heard her voice inside his head. It sent his senses into hyperdrive.

"Just don't let go."

Sam was holding his breath. Okay. So he definitely wasn't going to fall back to sleep. His stomach growled, and he tried to ignore it. Food was not an option. He was going to have to hide in here until she left for class.

He couldn't risk the possibility of seeing her in the skimpy T-shirt and sweats she always wore to eat breakfast. There was no telling what he might do.

* * *

Todd was still catching his breath as Professor Harbaugh announced the assignment for next week's class. People were already slamming their books shut and organizing their things when Todd slid into the hard plastic seat.

Nothing like being fashionably late, Todd thought, wondering how much he'd missed. The blackboards at the front of the lecture hall were covered with scrawled numbers and graphs. Perfect. And he didn't know a single person in this class, so there would be no copying of notes.

Sweat prickled the back of Todd's neck and his underarms from his mad, cross-campus dash, and he was sure he could already smell himself. Apparently he'd forgotten deodorant in his rush to get out of the apartment that morning. Sometimes the hot California sun was really not a good thing.

"Hold on, everyone," Harbaugh called out. "I have your papers graded." Half the class groaned, and the early risers lowered themselves back into their seats. Todd took the opportunity to relax for a minute.

Sure, the tow guy had told him his timing belt was broken and would take upward of a hundred and fifty dollars to fix. Sure, he'd taken the bus to SVU and run clear across campus in five minutes flat and still hadn't eaten a thing. That didn't change the fact that he'd aced this paper. Todd was sure of it. He'd worked his butt off.

His day was just about to get better.

As Harbaugh's teaching assistant started to return the papers at the front of the room, a notebook hit the floor behind Todd and slid under his seat. He picked it up, and when he turned around to hand it back to its owner, his heart skipped a beat. He was looking directly into the clear blue eyes of the girl he'd been checking out ever since he and his girlfriend, Dana, had broken up.

"Here you go," Todd said with a smile.

She smiled right back. "Thanks." She held his gaze for just a moment longer than necessary.

Yep. Things were definitely looking up.

Todd faced forward in his seat just as his paper was slapped onto his desk.

The heart that was skipping a moment ago took a nosedive onto the grungy linoleum floor.

D-plus?

Todd gripped the sides of his desk and quickly scanned the note scrawled next to the impossibly huge, red grade.

You have some well-thought-out ideas, but the assignment was to plan a strategy for a corporation, not a local nightclub.

All the blood from every extremity in his body rushed directly to Todd's face. He couldn't take a D on this paper. It was a quarter of his semester grade, and he'd worked really hard on it. Didn't effort count for anything around here?

Grabbing his bag and his paper, Todd fought the flow of traffic to get to the front of the room. Professor Harbaugh was snapping his briefcase shut and heading for the door.

"Professor?" Todd called out.

The short, stocky man stopped in his tracks, sighed irritably, and turned to face Todd. He had to tilt his balding head almost all the way back to do it.

"Yes, Mr. . . . ?"

"Wilkins," Todd said, trying not to sound too desperate. "Todd Wilkins. I wanted to talk to you about my grade."

Professor Harbaugh glanced at the D-plus and then looked Todd up and down as if he were an eyesore.

"Well, Mr. Wilkins, maybe if you'd granted me the courtesy of arriving at my class on time, I might sit down and discuss this with you," he said in a snide voice. "But if you don't feel the need to put in the time, neither do I."

Before Todd could even process what the man had just said, Professor Harbaugh was out the door, leaving Todd behind with a D-plus crumpled in his hand and his jaw on the floor.

Elizabeth Wakefield was trying really hard.

She'd spent the entire morning forcing her chin up. She'd worn her favorite light blue sweater. She'd spritzed herself with the expensive mood-enhancing perfume she'd gotten for her birthday. She'd even forced herself to hum while she was making coffee before she had to leave for campus. But so far, nothing had worked.

She was still as miserable as a wad of gum on the bottom of a hiking boot.

And that was why she was treating herself to breakfast out. Elizabeth forced herself to smile as she scanned the breakfast menu posted on the chalkboard behind the counter at the recently renovated Red Lion coffee shop. The specials were written out on the board in calligraphy with pastel-colored chalk. What could be better than this? The clatter of coffee mugs against saucers. The smell of frying bacon. The rustle of morning newspapers.

All she needed was a little good food, a little morning sunshine, and a little quality time with herself. As soon as she was settled into a booth, she'd be fine, and she wouldn't even think about . . . the guy she wasn't even going to think about.

"Yeah?" blurted out the tall brunette girl behind the counter, holding a pad and pen in front of her.

"I'll have an egg sandwich, a coffee, and half a grapefruit, please," Elizabeth said, barely maintaining her smile.

"And you're very happy about it, aren't you?"

12

the girl said sarcastically as she jotted down the order.

A deep blush rose to Elizabeth's cheeks as she waited in vain for the girl to either say she was kidding or apologize.

"That'll be four-fifty."

Elizabeth slapped a five into the girl's outstretched hand. She spent the next few minutes studiously avoiding eye contact as she waited for her food.

As soon as she had her tray in her hand, Elizabeth made a beeline for a booth that was both by a sunny window and as far away from the counter as possible.

Don't let her get to you, she thought as she settled into the vinyl-covered bench. *You don't even know her.*

Elizabeth hated how susceptible she was to embarrassment and insecurity when she was just getting over a breakup. It was like, just because some idiot guy hadn't really loved her after all, she felt as if she were totally worthless. She couldn't even stand up to that moron behind the counter just because Finn—

Finn.

Elizabeth's heart was in her shoes as the idiot guy in question, Finn Robinson, sauntered through the door of the café, a pretty Asian girl at his side. He looked perfect, of course, in pressed chinos and a light yellow oxford shirt, his freshly washed blond hair slicked back over his ears.

The words *don't let him see me* had barely formed in her mind when Finn's eyes were drawn to her like magnets. He blinked once, then smirked. A cocky, all-knowing smirk.

At that moment Elizabeth was about the size of a pea. Her ego was even smaller. She remembered how Finn had made her feel when she'd made the agonizing, confusing decision not to sleep with him. He'd called her a child.

She'd been sitting there, heart exposed, practically half her body exposed, more nervous than she'd ever been in her life . . .

And he'd laughed in her face. He'd been crueler than she would have believed possible of him.

Finn whispered something to the girl, never taking his eyes off Elizabeth. It took all the effort in the world to keep from puking all over her untouched food as he wove his way around chairs and customers and came to a stop at the end of her table.

"Hello, Elizabeth," he said.

The voice made the not puking even harder. She said nothing.

"Not talking to me, huh?" Finn said, a laugh in his tone. He casually pushed his hands into his pockets. "Well, that's very mature. Why am I not surprised?"

14

Elizabeth managed to look him in the eye, but that was it. He was hovering over her, and it was amazing what his self-assured posture and the demeaning look in his eyes could do. It rendered her mute. She felt like she'd been chucked out onstage in the middle of a play and she hadn't learned a single line.

Say something! her mind screamed. *Anything! Just say anything!* But her brain was so busy making impossible demands, it didn't leave room for snappy-comeback manufacturing.

Suddenly Elizabeth was on her feet. She had to sidestep around Finn. There was no way he was actually going to be a gentleman and give her space. She'd made it halfway across the room before the tears sprang to her eyes. She blinked them back with a well of effort.

"Oh, c'mon, Liz, don't go!" Finn said loudly. "You didn't finish your kiddie meal."

And with that, Elizabeth burst into tears and pushed through the plate-glass door.

Chapter Two

"Hey, man, thanks," Neil Martin said, reaching out to slap hands with Sam. "Professor Flutie would have flunked me if I was late. I owe you one." He climbed out of the car and pulled his silver-and-gray messenger bag over his shoulder.

"Yeah?" Sam asked as Neil slammed the door. "How about five bucks? I'm starving, and I have no cash."

Neil flashed a grin and fished his wallet out of the back pocket of his jeans. "Least I could do after bumming a ride and rushing you out of the house before you could scarf your precious Froot Loops."

He chucked a ten-dollar bill through the open passenger-side window. It fluttered down and hit the seat. "There's ten," Neil said, slapping the top of the car. "Buy yourself something nice."

Sam laughed. "Thanks! Later, man!" He swung the car into a parking space as Neil headed off to class.

Now the question was, where could he grab some grub? Sam climbed out of the car and checked his surroundings. He didn't go to SVU, so he wasn't all that familiar with the campus. For the most part he only knew how to get to the bars where his friends sometimes took him to hang out.

He started to stroll along the sidewalk, rolling his eyes at a group of guys in cargo shorts and no shirts who were playing Frisbee on a huge lawn. It was such a cliché. Like anyone ever played Frisbee *before* they got to college.

Suddenly the smell of scrambled eggs and the sweet aroma of maple syrup arrested Sam's attention. His stomach grumbled loudly, and he looked up to check the source of the smell. Unfortunately he was standing in front of the huge, stucco-walled dining hall. No student meal card, no scrambled eggs.

An obvious freshman in a plaid shirt walked by quickly with his head down. "Hey," Sam said, causing the kid to flinch and look up warily. "Do you know where I can snag a hot breakfast around here?"

Mr. Freshman looked at Sam wide-eyed for a moment before finally answering. "The Red Lion," he said quietly, pointing across the quad. "It's sort of a diner."

"Thanks, man," Sam said. He stuffed his hands in the front pockets of his baggy jeans and took off at a brisk walk, cutting through the triangle of Frisbee players. The maneuver solicited a few yells, but Sam's mind was on other things. He knew exactly what he was going to get with Neil's ten dollars. Bacon, eggs, pancakes, hash browns, extra wheat toast, and a huge glass of orange juice. When he was just a few yards away from the breakfast of his dreams, the door to the Red Lion flew open, and Elizabeth ran out.

She was bawling.

Any trace of hunger disappeared and was replaced by a dull ache. What had happened to Little Miss Morning Musical? Sam was about to go after her when a flash of dirty-blond hair caught his eye. He knew who it was before his eyes even focused on the form sitting down by the window.

The ex-fabulous Finn Robinson.

Then there was nothing but the rush of adrenaline. What had that egotistical waste of space done to Elizabeth now?

Sam's hands balled into fists. There was no reason to stand around wondering when he could just find out for himself.

Sam thrust open the glass door to the Red Lion and walked directly over to Finn's table. Finn actually smiled when he saw Sam coming. He took

19

a long sip of coffee and lowered the ceramic mug onto the table, looking up at Sam's enraged face the entire time.

"What the hell is your problem?" Sam said evenly, amazed at himself for sounding semicalm.

"Well, if it isn't the loyal roomie," Finn said, leaning back in his seat and draping his arm across the top of the bench. "What can I do for you?"

Sam planted one hand on the surface of the table and leaned in toward Finn's face. Finn adjusted his position only slightly, obviously trying to look unaffected by Sam's menacing stance.

"You can leave Elizabeth alone," Sam said, his eyes boring into Finn's.

Finn glanced sideways, then refocused on Sam. The guy actually smirked. "I really don't think that's going to be a problem," he said.

"Um, excuse me?"

At the sound of a female voice behind him, Sam straightened up and turned slightly. There was a pretty Chinese girl standing beside him, holding a tray full of food. Enough for both her and Finn. She looked up at Sam questioningly with just the slightest bit of apprehension in her eyes. So this was the next victim. Lovely.

Sam looked at Finn again. His face was so smug, Sam came dangerously close to driving his fist directly into Finn's teeth. But he couldn't do that. Too messy. And he might hurt his own hand. Dr. Not So

Cool wasn't worth the risk of personal injury.

"Remember what I said, man," Sam warned, turning as if he were going to walk away. Instead he quickly, deftly lifted the side of the table across from Finn, causing the mug of hot coffee to slide directly into Finn's lap.

"Aaaaauuuugggggghhhh!" Finn screamed, jumping up and slamming his knees against the underside of the table. He started blurting out a stream of curses as he yanked napkins from the dispenser on the table next to his.

Sam smiled at the Chinese girl, who was staring dumbfounded at her breakfast date. "Stay away from him. Trust me," Sam told her, glancing at Finn, who was now fanning his nether regions with a plastic menu.

Sam made his way out of the café, leaving the diners either staring or laughing after him. The feeling of triumph was almost enough to make him forget that he still hadn't gotten his hands on a single morsel of food.

At least he knew Finn wouldn't be getting frisky with any more underclassmen for a few days.

"Egotistical idiot!" Todd muttered, crumpling his marketing paper into a tight ball as he stormed out of the business-school building. As he descended the concrete steps, he pulled back his arm to toss his paper into the bushes.

"Kind of upset about your grade, huh?"

Todd froze in mid windup. For some reason, the voice sent a pleasant shiver down his spine, even though it was completely unfamiliar.

He turned around to find the blue-eyed girl from his class strolling toward him. She was wearing standard early morning class gear—gray sweats and a little black T-shirt with a pair of comfy-looking sneakers. Her curly brown hair was back in a pony-tail that was pulled through the back of a well-worn SVU baseball cap. Todd had never seen anyone make sweats look so good.

Of course, he looked like he'd just been hit by a Mack truck. Twice.

"Yeah," Todd said, lowering his arm and straightening his untucked shirt. A slight blush rose to his face as he realized how immature he must look. He quickly stuffed the balled-up paper into the back pocket on his knapsack. "I'm not having a good morning," he said, hoping to ex-plain away his over-the-top reaction.

"Yeah, me neither," the girl said with a gri-mace. She held up her own paper. It had a big, red C-plus in the corner and no other comment. What Todd wouldn't have given to be in her place. "I'm Jodi," the girl said, holding out her hand. "Fellow Harbaugh sufferer."

Todd grinned. Up until now all he'd known was that she was good-looking and she never came to class without a large, pungent, French vanilla coffee. It was nice to know she had a sense of humor.

"Todd," he said. "And if it helps, I swear I'm suffering worse."

Jodi laughed, and it brightened her entire face. "So, do you want to commiserate on our common misery over breakfast at the dining hall?" She raised her eyebrows flirtatiously. Both Todd's heart and his stomach responded. One with a little leap and the other with a grumble.

He looked at the ground, hoping he wasn't about to blow it completely. "I'd love to," he said, shoving his hands into his pockets. "But I've got another class across campus, so . . ."

"Oh," Jodi said. She crossed her arms over her chest and scuffed at the ground with her sneaker. "Okay."

Todd felt his nerves start to fray. She thought he was rejecting her. *C'mon, man,* he thought. *This might be your last chance to turn this day around.*

"But I'd love to . . . commiserate on our common misery over dinner," he said, tucking his chin in an attempt to catch her eye.

She looked up and smiled but didn't stop scuffing. Definitely wondering whether or not he was sincere.

"How about Thursday night?" Todd asked with a casual smile. "That should give us long enough to recover from our bad grades."

Jodi nodded once, her curls bouncing. "Sounds good." She fished a pen out of her bag and ripped the C-plus from the corner of her paper. Then she leaned against Todd's shoulder and wrote her number on the back of the scrap.

"Give me a call," she said, holding the paper out between two fingers.

Todd snapped it out of her grasp and grinned. "I definitely will," he said.

"See ya." Smiling, Jodi turned on her heel and sauntered away. She waved once over her shoulder, and it was all Todd could do to keep from laughing. The mashed marketing paper was all but forgotten. After weeks of stealing glances at the beautiful blue-eyed girl, he finally had a name . . . and a number.

This day was definitely looking up.

"This can't be happening to me," Nina Harper muttered as she slowly descended the stone steps outside Murray Hall. In her hands, she gripped her latest biochemistry lab exam—the one with the C-minus on it. The second C-minus she'd gotten in the last week. Up until now Nina had thought C's were reserved for deadheads, slackers, guys with names like Shred.

Losers.

Now she was one of them.

The writing on the paper blurred as Nina's eyes filled with humiliated tears.

No. Not possible. She shook her head as she shuffled along, her high-heeled boots sliding noisily on the grainy pavement, her always hefty book bag feeling like it had gained fifty pounds. A few of her classmates shot her strange, semiconcerned, semiamused looks as they scurried away to their next classes. With shaky hands Nina flipped through the crinkled pages of her exam as she walked, scanning the contents. She almost slammed into a professor who was running to class, but she didn't even look up.

"Wait a minute—*what?*" Nina blurted out, reading through her notes on the laboratory procedure. They were completely muddled and undetailed—and copying down the procedure was the easiest part. There were typos everywhere, and she'd even spelled the word *cell* wrong a few times.

"*S-e-l-l?*" Nina said aloud, lowering herself blindly onto a bench and dropping her bag onto the ground with a thud. Suddenly she wasn't so indignant anymore. In fact, she was surprised that her professor hadn't drop-kicked her back to elementary school.

A mortified blush spread across Nina's chocolate brown skin as a light breeze lifted her dark hair from her shoulders. She read over the rest of the exam, the warmth in her face growing stronger with every word. She was pathetic. God, she was *lucky* to have pulled a C.

"Hey! Wake up, girl!"

Nina blinked a few times and looked up to find three cute guys chuckling as they walked past her. One of them winked as they jogged away, but Nina wasn't remotely amused. She must have looked like a zombie, sitting there staring into space.

Still, cute boy number one did have a point. He was rude and forward, but he did have a point. Nina grabbed her backpack and stuffed the offending paper inside.

"That's the last C I'm ever going to get," she told herself as she swung her bag onto her shoulder. What was she thinking, letting her classes slide while she went out and partied and flirted every night? There was no way she could spend 70 percent of her time in bars and clubs and guys' rooms and still pull decent grades. And without decent grades, Nina had no self-respect.

And without self-respect, Nina Harper was nothing.

Pulling her tiny denim jacket tightly around her torso, Nina bent her head and started across campus at a fast clip. She was going right back to the dorm to study. There would be no TV. No phone calls. No distractions whatso—

"Nina!"

Uh-oh.

A little voice inside Nina's head told her to keep walking. To just ignore him, but her eyes didn't obey, and she glanced up at the door of Yum-Yum's, one of the campus cafés.

Sure enough, Xavier was standing in the doorway, dreadlocks framing his light brown skin, smile lighting up just about the entire world.

"Hey, sweetness," he said, causing her insides to turn to goo. "Come in and have breakfast with us."

Nina glanced through the window and saw a few of the members of Xavier's band, Wired, sitting around a table and chowing down on pancakes and eggs.

"I can't," Nina said. *Good girl*, the inner voice answered.

"C'mon," Xavier cajoled, tilting his head. "The food here is deadly."

Nina eyed Xavier's friend Bones as he crammed a forkful of Belgian waffle into his mouth. It did look *really* good.

Her eyes darted back to Xavier. Breakfast didn't look half as good as Xavier did in his bright red FUBU T-shirt and his little beaded necklace that she'd nearly broken in a fit of passion just last night.

Nina blushed at the memory.

What could one little meal hurt? She had to eat, right?

No! Remember the C-minus! Remember the humiliation.

Yeah? Well, remember last night, Nina murmured silently. *Last night was worth two C-minuses.*

She gagged the inner voice and practically skipped through the door of Yum-Yum's.

In the student-center bathroom Todd splashed some water on his face and stared at his reflection in the dull, scratched mirror.

"Wow," he said to himself in his so-tired-I'm-hoarse voice. "You look ugly, my friend."

Part of the problem with living off campus was not being able to run home between classes and shower. It forced one to resort to many heinous acts—like washing one's face with the harsh, pink liquid soap they kept in the bathrooms, using paper towels that were hard enough to tile the floor to dab the moisture from one's underarms, and chewing cinnamon gum in place of toothpaste to freshen one's skanky breath.

Todd straightened up as best his tired back could handle and took a long breath. It was time to go home. Of course, he wouldn't be there for over an hour because he was going to have to take the crawling bus all the way across town.

Suddenly Todd realized his head was hanging, and he squared his shoulders again. Might as well get it over with.

He swung open the heavy wooden door with a creak and walked directly into some guy's shoulder. Some guy's very solid shoulder.

The apology was on the tip of Todd's tongue

when he took a step back and focused on the face that belonged to the shoulder in question. In an instant his aching back become ramrod straight and his sleep-deprived fogginess evaporated.

It was Tom Watts. And he was surrounded by three of his doofier-looking football teammates.

"Wilkins," Tom said, stepping back and raising his chin slightly. It gave Todd a little rush every time he realized how much taller he was than Mr. Football Superstar. There was nothing more intimidating than height advantage.

"Watts," he said, maintaining steady eye contact.

Tom Watts. The intellectual wuss turned sleazy superjock who had slept with Dana, effectively causing their breakup. Todd had never wanted to hit anyone so much in his life. And from the tension crackling between them, he was sure Tom knew what he was thinking. On some level Tom had to know he deserved a good pummeling. You didn't just sleep with a guy's girlfriend and expect no retaliation.

But Todd made it a strict policy never to throw the first punch. Man, he wished Tom would just brush him with his pinkie. That would be all he needed.

Tom was staring him down, or staring him *up*, more accurately, and Todd wasn't about to budge. As immature as it was, he wasn't going to let Tom get away with screwing up Todd's most promising relationship to date *and* let the guy beat him in a staring match in front of his friends.

"Tom, man. Let's go," one of the meatheads said. Todd wasn't sure which one because he wasn't about to shift his eyes.

Finally Tom backed away slightly and looked Todd up and down.

Yes! Todd thought. *Victory is mine!* He almost blushed at the twelve-year-old mentality of it all.

"Yeah," Tom said. "Let's not go there, huh, Wilkins?"

Todd's jaw clenched as he tried to think of something to say in response, but nothing came to him, and he was forced to let Tom have the last word. He stood there and watched as Captain Football and his friends skulked off, whistling and catcalling at a couple of freshman girls as they went.

The girls, of course, blushed and giggled and grabbed each other's wrists. If this had been the seventeenth century, everyone would have had to whip out their smelling salts. All for a bunch of boneheads who probably couldn't even spell the word *swoon*.

Todd's adrenaline rush morphed into pure ire. He turned and trudged out of the student center, throwing open the door so hard, it slammed back against the wall. He hated this school. Hated everything about it. From the pompous teachers to the crappy bus system to the lousy soap in the bathrooms.

And he hated the damn shallow girls.

As Todd speed walked down the street toward the bus stop, he realized he was itching to get to Frankie's tonight. He wanted to wash all the snobbery he'd been immersed in for the past few hours off his psyche. Then he remembered he wasn't scheduled to work until the next day.

Damn, he thought, waiting for a car full of butt-smoking frat boys to make a turn so he could cross the street.

Maybe he'd go to Frankie's tonight to hang out anyway. He just couldn't handle the thought of sitting alone in his apartment after an ego-bruising day like this. *Hey, wait a minute,* he thought. *I'm forgetting about Jodi. She totally came on to me. So today hasn't been a total bust.*

Todd silently told the frat boys that they were big, fat losers, then smiled and crossed the street.

Chapter Three

Before Sam was even out the door of Dee Jay's, the music store downtown, he'd popped open his new Dave Matthews Band CD to check the liner notes. As always, Dave and friends did not disappoint. All the words to every song. Sam didn't know why more bands didn't provide their fans with their poetry so they could sing along.

Stuffing the CD back in the red plastic bag, Sam ventured out onto tree-lined Cypress Avenue. It was a perfect day—a perfect day to be skipping class and window-shopping like he was right now. And if he wanted to avoid the duplex, which he did at that moment, he couldn't have asked for better weather. There wasn't a cloud in the sky, and a light breeze kept the midday air from getting too warm.

A beautiful redhead in a tank top and practically-underwear-short shorts sauntered by and smiled at

Sam, letting her eyes roam over his body for an extended moment. Sam smiled back and took a deep breath of the salty California air. It was good to be him.

Suddenly a couple of girls about his age burst out onto the sidewalk in front of him, giggling and talking a mile a minute. Sam stopped to let them pass. They kept grabbing each other's shopping bags and checking out the contents.

"Omigod! She'll totally *love* that!" one of them squealed, pulling a little candle votive out of a bag.

"Yeah, but wait till she sees what *you* got her!" the other girl answered as they scurried around the corner.

"Sorority chicks," Sam muttered. He stuffed one hand in the pocket of his pants, groping around for his keys, but the sign outside the sorority-girl store caught his eye.

It was a large wooden sign hanging from an iron pole, and it was swinging in the breeze with the tiniest of creaks. Carved into the wood were the letters *ETC*, and there were vines carved all around them. Sam's eyebrows knitted together. Where had he seen that before?

A woman stepped out, carrying a brown paper bag with the same logo, and Sam suddenly had a rush of memory. He'd seen the same bag in Elizabeth's hand last week while she'd been babbling to Jessica about how great the store was.

Something about wanting to buy everything in it. Of course. She was such a girl.

You're smiling again, his internal voice chided. Sam felt a slight blush coming on and squelched it, glancing left and right to make sure no one had caught him daydreaming. There was, in fact, a little old woman gazing at him warily as she toddled by, holding her purse a little bit closer to herself. Trying to look like he had a purpose, Sam tugged at the tattered bill of his baseball cap and ducked inside the store.

The first thing that hit him was the smell. Sweet and spicy aromas arrested his senses the moment he stepped through the door, giving the air a comforting, heavy feel. Glancing around, Sam realized one wall was lined with all colors, sizes, and shapes of candles and even more styles of candleholders—beaded, glass, silver, iron, wooden. The shelves were totally unorganized, as if the owner expected the customers to feel free to spend hours browsing.

Sam caught the young girl behind the counter staring at him quizzically, so he walked down an aisle. Instantly he knew why Elizabeth loved this store. She could have stocked the place from her bedroom. There were all kinds of funky journals—some covered in velvet, others made from handmade paper, others bound with leather. There were magnets, frames, rugs, pencils and pens, inspirational posters, artsy jewelry, boxes, bags, and all kinds of earthy-yet-girlish stuff.

No wonder the salesgirl was staring at him. She probably thought he'd taken a wrong turn on his way back from the hardware store.

Sam was about to turn on his heel and flee when he spotted a jar full of pencils that had cartoon characters hugging the ends. He picked up a red Bugs Bunny pencil and smirked. Elizabeth watched that ancient cartoon show every Saturday when she thought no one was looking. She'd probably love the thing.

Once again Sam found himself smiling stupidly, imagining the way Elizabeth's face would light up if she came home and found some silly little gift in her room. The other night, when he'd picked her up after Finn had dumped her, all Sam could think about was finding a way to make Elizabeth smile again. Make her stop hurting so much.

And then the guy went and made her miserable all over again, Sam thought, clutching his CD bag so hard, the plastic started to stick to his palm. He couldn't wipe the memory of Elizabeth fleeing the Red Lion in tears from his mind. The girl needed cheering up now more than ever.

Sam took the pencil and returned to a shelf full of journals. Scanning the covers, he quickly selected a fuzzy red book that matched the pencil and had no lines on the pages. That way she could write as tiny or as huge as she wanted. Sam, for one, knew that when he was pissed off, his writing came out a jagged mess. A journal should leave a person free to vent like that.

As he grabbed the journal and headed for the register, Sam had a sinking feeling in his gut, and he slowed his pace. What was he doing? Gift buying definitely sent a signal, and he really wasn't sure if he was signal ready.

"Can I help you?" the girl behind the counter asked, an amused smile playing about her lips.

"Yeah," Sam said, determinedly placing the pencil and journal on the counter. There was no way he was going to walk out of here without those things and let this girl think he was too much of a wuss to buy them.

Besides, Elizabeth was always there for everyone whenever they needed her. She deserved someone to return the favor.

Signals or not.

"Okay, so the bus is never going to come," Todd muttered, rubbing his hand over his tired eyes. "Just accept it and move on with your life."

Todd had been waiting at the stop on the edge of campus for a little over half an hour, getting more and more tired and more and more ready to call in a bomb threat to the bus company. He glanced up the busy road. Should he try to walk it? His feet responded with an irritated pang even at the thought. Okay. Maybe he should try to hitch.

"Hey, Todd! Need a ride?"

Never had more beautiful words been uttered.

Todd glanced up to see Elizabeth Wakefield, apparently the angel of mercy, idling her Jeep in front of the bus stop. Every muscle in Todd's body instantly relaxed. *Thank you for old friends.*

"You have no idea how much," he said, popping open the passenger-side door and climbing inside. "Thanks for stopping. I live, like, a half hour away from campus now, though. Lincoln Ave. You don't mind going out of your way?"

Elizabeth shook her head and pulled the car out onto the road, and Todd couldn't believe how relieved he felt just to be moving. "It's no problem," Elizabeth said.

An alarm bell instantly went off in Todd's head at the sound of her voice. It was all throaty and tired. He turned and looked fully at her face for the first time and noticed her nose was slightly red and her eyes were an even brighter blue-green than usual.

"Liz? Have you been crying?" Todd asked carefully.

"No," she said. But he knew that tone from years of experience. It was a yes-but-I-don't-want-you-to-know no.

38

"Does this have anything to do with that whole Sam thing last Saturday night?" Todd asked as she took a corner just a tad too fast. "I mean, I hope I didn't do anything wrong, but when he asked me to confirm that the guy you were with at the party was the same one who'd been all over some girl at Frankie's—"

"So, how's everything with you, Todd?" Elizabeth asked with a smile so tight, it could have been Ziploc sealed.

It was an extremely abrupt topic shift, so Todd just decided to go with it. He knew Elizabeth would talk if she wanted to. And she usually wanted to, so if she was clamming up, it had to be pretty bad.

Luckily he had a subject that would undoubt-edly distract her brain. "Well, I'm thinking about dropping out for the rest of the semester. Maybe next semester too," Todd said, and suddenly he was face-to-face with a mailbox as Elizabeth almost drove off the road.

"What the hell are you doing?" Todd blurted out, his hands pressing against the dash as she righted the car.

"You're thinking about *what?*" she demanded, glancing at him with almost wild eyes.

"Don't sound so disturbed," Todd said, now watching the road carefully. "My job at Frankie's is great. The people are really cool, I'm learning a

39

lot, and I'm making good money. If I'm happier there and I can support myself, I don't really see the point of staying in school. I'm down to two classes as it is."

Elizabeth swung another hard right and came to a lurching stop in a parking space on some street. She threw the car in park, unbuckled her seat belt, and turned completely sideways in her seat to look at him.

"You . . . have lost . . . your mind," she said, with way too much drama.

Todd felt anger start to bubble up in his veins for about the hundredth time that day. "Wait a minute—"

"Have you even *thought* about this?" Elizabeth interrupted, leaning forward slightly. "You're going to work in a *bar* for a living?" She said it as if she were talking about hanging out with cockroaches. "What about your parents? What about your future? Do you really think you can live like you're used to living working in some locals' club? I mean—"

"*First* of all," Todd interrupted harshly, causing Elizabeth's mouth to snap shut. "Where the hell do you get off telling me how to live my life? It's not like it's mattered to you at all in the past, oh, I don't know, *year*."

Elizabeth's eyes narrowed, and her whole face went pink, but Todd wasn't about to stop. It felt

40

good to finally let out all the rage and exhausted indignation he'd been feeling all day. "And second, I know that hanging out with a back-bar guy isn't the same as fraternizing with future *doctors* and all, but at least I'm a good person and not some egotistical jackass who cheats on his girlfriend."

Elizabeth didn't move a muscle, but Todd could see the flinch in her eyes. "Get . . . out . . . of my . . . car."

Todd felt an inkling of regret, but not enough to even put a dent in his armor. As if *she* hadn't insulted *him* first. "Gladly," he said, scrambling out and slamming the door behind him.

Before he could even turn around, Elizabeth peeled out—probably for the first time in her goody-goody life—and left Todd seething on the sidewalk.

"What a total snot," Todd said, turning on his heel. He was glad he still had a ten-minute walk home—he could use it to work off some of his anger.

By the time he reached his apartment building, he was even more furious at Elizabeth. Todd never would have thought it of Elizabeth, but she was just the same as every other snobby girl at SVU—looking down at him for the high crime of holding down a job and going to school only part-time. What a *lowlife* he was!

Todd flung open the door and headed up the stairs, taking them two at a time. Maybe they'd all prefer it if he were a no-brain jock, or a male slut, or a girlfriend stealer. Maybe they'd all prefer it if he had no life, just like all the other guys on campus.

As he noisily, clumsily opened the door to his apartment, Todd had one last, disturbing thought. Was it even remotely possible that Jodi could be the one girl on campus who *wouldn't* look down on him?

Todd closed the door and pulled off his shirt, dropping it behind him as he headed directly for the shower.

I hope so, he thought, imagining Jodi's smiling face. *I really hope so.*

"Jess!" Elizabeth yelled, storming into the house and swinging the door shut behind her. "Jessica!" She stalked over to the stairs, her temples still throbbing from her argument with Todd, and yelled again. "Jess!"

There was no answer. There was nothing but the sound of the kitchen sink dripping into the ever present pile of dirty dishes.

"Dammit!" Elizabeth spat, flinging her book bag onto the floor. Why was Jessica never around when she wanted to vent?

Grabbing the portable phone from the coffee table, Elizabeth dropped down onto the couch and crossed her legs, her foot bouncing up and down as she dialed. Where did Todd get off, talking to her that way? He knew less than nothing about her life. And he had no right to comment on her relationship with Finn. Or her lack thereof.

The phone line rang for the third time, and Elizabeth heard the familiar sound of Nina's machine picking up. "Hey! Leave a message, and I'll call you back as soon as—"

Elizabeth hit the off button and tossed the phone to the other end of the couch. "Yeah, right, you'll call back as soon as your new life permits," she muttered.

Taking a deep breath, Elizabeth pressed both hands against her forehead and dropped back her head. She couldn't believe the violence of her reaction to Todd. This wasn't like her. Usually she could let other people's opinions roll off her back like nothing. Why did this whole Finn thing get to her so much?

Opening her eyes again, Elizabeth glanced around the eerily quiet living room, suddenly feeling about as heavy as a truckload of bowling balls. Her body was done with the anger, and the post-adrenaline crash was draining the life right out of her. She considered the television for a moment but didn't even feel like she had the energy to lift the remote or to put in the meager brainpower required to watch a bad soap opera.

She had studying to do, but her books were all the way across the room, and that *definitely* wasn't going to happen.

Finally her eyes fell on the phone again, and out of nowhere, all she wanted to do was call Finn.

She wanted to call him and yell at him for making her feel this way. For making her feel stupid and naive and for making her a laughingstock to her friends. She wanted to ask him why he'd done it to her. What she'd ever done to deserve it.

Elizabeth's hand slowly traveled to the phone. She picked it up and stared at the little gray buttons with the little white numbers on them, Finn's digits reciting themselves in her mind.

Then she tried to lift her thumb from the side of the receiver and realized it was stuck. Elizabeth's face scrunched up in disgust. What *was* that?

Turning the phone over in her hand, she saw that there was a semifresh smear of grape jelly on the side.

"Ugh, Sam," Elizabeth grumbled, putting the phone down again.

Sam.

What would he say if he knew she was considering calling Finn? Elizabeth slouched down on the couch, pressing her head back into the soft, velvety cushion. He'd definitely tell her she was nuts. That calling Finn, even to tell him off, would make her look hysterical—like she cared too much about what he'd done. It would just give him the upper hand.

Elizabeth stared at an old nail hole in the wall that they'd never bothered to cover up. Sam had said he'd deal with it a hundred times, and he'd never even gotten around to buying the Spackle. For weeks Jessica had railed on about how useless he was—not that Jessica had ever bothered to deal with it herself.

But Sam wasn't worthless. In fact, Elizabeth would have given anything at that moment just to have him sitting next to her on the couch. As a listener and a friend, Sam had turned out to be worth a lot. Even when he wasn't here, the thought of him was preventing her from making an idiot of herself.

Elizabeth took all the throw pillows on the couch and covered the phone with them just to keep her from being tempted. Then she got up and went to the kitchen to search out the pint of Ben & Jerry's she'd hidden in the back of the freezer.

By the time she was halfway done with it, Sam would be home from his afternoon classes and she would be able to talk to him in person. Elizabeth grinned as she pushed aside a box of pizza rolls and some freezer-burned chicken and grabbed her ice cream.

She couldn't wait to tell Sam about her near cave-in and how she'd gotten past it. She couldn't wait to thank him.

Once Todd realized he'd read the same sentence approximately fifty-five times, he slammed his marketing book closed and tossed it onto his bed. No matter what he did to make himself concentrate—covering the television with a blanket, downing caffeinated coffee, cleaning his room from top to bottom—Todd just couldn't seem to keep his brain on his books. It was like he'd developed a chemical rejection of all things college.

Unfortunately some of what Elizabeth had said earlier had started to sink in. Todd still didn't appreciate the condescending way in which she'd said it, but it kind of made sense. Did he really see himself as a career bartender? Would his kids, if he ever had kids, be proud of their beer-peddling dad? And of course, the most convincing of arguments—his parents would definitely kill him.

Groaning, Todd reached over one of his extremely long arms and picked up his book again.

"Okay," he said, grabbing his pen and smoothing his hand over a new sheet of paper in his notebook. "Chapter three, 'Marketing in the New Market.'" Todd chuckled. These textbook writers were just such kooky, creative guys.

Todd started to read the first sentence—for the fifty-sixth time.

In order to be competitive in today's marketplace, companies must constantly be searching for the next big thing. The next trend that will blow the market wide open—

Gradually Todd's eyes unfocused, and he found himself staring at a bunch of blurred ink. New ideas. What a shockingly brilliant observation. New ideas, good. Old ideas, bad. This was definitely knowledge worth spending his parents' hard-earned money on.

New ideas. Todd had a few of his own, but they had nothing to do with big-business marketing. He had ideas for Frankie's. Todd leaned back in his rickety desk chair and crooked his arms behind his head.

There was this radio station in LA that was constantly sponsoring dance contests at clubs all over the city. Todd figured they might like to do a college-theme show and come up to SVU. If Frankie's held the contest and it was promoted correctly, they could definitely bring in a ton of kids from campus. They could get the word out that Frankie's wasn't the townie dive everyone thought it was.

Of course, pulling in the college kids could have its drawbacks. It would no longer be a respite from the SVU obnoxiousness. Maybe it would be better to stick to things that appealed to the kind of crowd that already hung out there. Foosball contests. Football pools. Wet T-shirt contests.

Todd laughed out loud, slammed his book shut again, and clicked off his desk lamp. He quickly rummaged through his bag and pulled out his marketing paper, then grabbed his jacket and headed for the door.

There was no point in sitting here not studying something he would never use or even comprehend. He already had ideas that could be put to use in the real world.

Chapter
Four

Nina grinned giddily as Xavier danced his way back from the bathroom at Starlights on Monday night. She was sandwiched in between Bones and some guy named Chaz who came complete with a girlfriend attached to him at the lip. The bar was smoky, loud, hot, and uncomfortable, but watching Xavier made her smile.

Everything about Xavier made her smile.

He carried two bottles of beer as he half moshed, half boogied his way through the crowd.

"Up," Xavier said to Bones when he reached the table.

"Whatever, dude," Bones said, rising unsteadily off the bench so Xavier could have the approximately three inches of space next to Nina. As soon as Xavier sat down, Bones plopped down next to him on the other side, and his head hit the table.

"Are you okay?" Nina asked, staring at the spot where Bones's cheek had mashed an already broken peanut shell. He didn't answer her. In fact, all he did was snore.

Xavier glanced at his friend. "He's down for the count," he said with a slow grin. Normally Nina would be worried about anyone who had drunk themselves into a near coma, but Xavier's smile excited the overtired butterflies in her stomach, and all she could see was him.

Suddenly Nina was jostled from behind, and there was a painful jab to her spine. She turned around to find Chaz and his girlfriend mauling each other. They were so oblivious, they didn't even realize they were practically reclining on Nina.

"Hey! I'm kind of sitting here," she said. They just kept right on spit swapping.

Xavier trailed a finger delicately down her cheek, recommending Nina's attention. When she turned to look at him, his face was centimeters away.

"Looks to me like they have the right idea," Xavier said, bringing his lips to hers in a quick but intensely sensual kiss. Nina wasn't one for PDAs, but she could have jumped him right then and there. Who knew what she'd been missing by spending all those hours in the library last year?

"Last round!" a waitress yelled as she walked by. "Order up now! Last round!"

Nina blinked and pushed Xavier away before he could plant another mind-altering kiss on her. "What does she mean, last round?" Nina blurted out. "What time is it?"

Xavier heaved a sigh and took a swig of his beer. "I don't know. You know I don't feel the need for a watch."

Reaching over him, Nina grabbed Bones's limp arm and twisted it so she could see the face on his digital watch. Her heart felt as if it were being sucked into the floor by a vacuum.

"One forty-five?" she practically shouted. She looked at Xavier, her mouth hanging open, her fingers still clasping Bones's arm. "In the *morning?*"

Xavier laughed and swigged his beer again. "We've been here for, like, ever," he said, his eyes roaming the crowd. "What's wrong?"

Nina kicked at her book bag, which was under her feet on the grimy bar floor. She hadn't even thought about it since that morning when she'd met up with Xavier for breakfast. Since then she'd gone back to his house to watch the band rehearse, driven to the beach for what Bones called the best tortillas in the known universe, hung out at an arcade on the boardwalk, grabbed a catnap at Xavier's, and then ended up here. All day she'd been telling herself that she still had time to study. How did it get to be almost two A.M.?

"C'mon, baby," Xavier said, leaning forward

and tickling her neck with his breath. Nina closed her eyes as chills slid down her spine. "Don't stress. There's nothing you can do about it now."

"You have a point," Nina said, tilting her head back slightly as Xavier trailed kisses up the side of her neck and behind her ear. He knew exactly where he had to kiss her to make her brain go foggy so that she forgot everything but the sensation. She'd known him just a week, and already he knew this about her. He was really good.

Nina turned her face toward his and caught his mouth in a long, lingering kiss. The music, the smoke, and even Chaz and his tonsil-hockey partner faded into the background. All she knew was Xavier.

Finally Xavier broke away and leaned his forehead against hers. His eyes were closed, and he was breathing heavily. Nina smiled as her heart pounded along with his breath.

"What do you say we skip last round and go back to your room?" he suggested, opening his eyes for a moment and meeting her gaze. Nina's heart skipped a beat at his closeness.

"Don't have to ask me twice," she said.

Xavier went about rousing Bones from his stupor as Nina fished under the table for the strap on her backpack. As she hoisted it onto her shoulder, she felt another twinge of guilt. Hadn't she just made a pact with herself to be more responsible?

Maybe she should tell Xavier to go home and then try to get some studying in before she passed out.

But as Xavier reached out and took her hand, Nina's conscience disappeared. It was too late to concentrate on theorems and theories and themes.

But it was never too late to concentrate on a guy like Xavier.

Elizabeth rolled over in bed and slapped her hand down on top of her unsuspecting alarm clock, silencing the invasive, persistent beeping. She couldn't believe it was already morning. She'd spent half the night staring at the red, digital numbers, wondering why time seemed to pass so slowly when she had insomnia. Then, what seemed like about five seconds later, there she was being jolted awake by the alarm.

Rubbing the back of her hand over her eyes, Elizabeth slowly sat up. Her head felt like it weighed twice as much as the rest of her body.

She'd probably had about three hours of sleep—all of them restless. No matter what she had done the night before, she couldn't stop thinking about Finn. She'd concentrated with all her brainpower on her usual fall-asleep games. Like naming a movie for each letter of the alphabet or counting backward from 999. Every time she thought she was doing well, she'd suddenly realize she'd stopped naming or counting and images of Finn and the mortifying night they'd almost spent together had permeated her brain without her even noticing.

With more effort than she could possibly spare, Elizabeth swung her legs over the side of her bed and trudged to the door. *Coffee,* she thought groggily as her bare feet slapped against the hardwood floor. *Must have coffee.*

She reached for the doorknob, missing it twice in her dopey-eyed stupor, and finally swung open the door. Something dropped at her feet, and Elizabeth pulled her foot back just in time before she stepped on the foreign object.

"What the—," she muttered, blinking to clear away the remnants of sleep. Her eyebrows knit together as she crouched to the floor. She picked up a book with a furry red cover and a little Bugs Bunny pencil that was lying next to it. Confused, Elizabeth turned the book over in her hand. No card. No note. Nothing.

She opened the cover and blinked. Hard.

There, in black ink on the red page that divided the cover from the blank journal pages, was a note. It read: *Thought you could use this. —Sam.*

"Yeah, right," Elizabeth said, looking over her shoulder as if someone were going to jump out of the closet to announce the practical joke. Her room was empty.

She glanced back at the book again, and the

note was actually there. She would have pinched herself to see if she was dreaming, but she knew she hadn't fallen into a deep enough sleep for dreams.

Reading the note again, Elizabeth's heart swelled and tears filled her eyes, as if her heart had pumped them there to get rid of its overflow. Sam had bought her a gift? Sam *Burgess*?

"Thought you could use this," she repeated, closing the door and letting the tears overflow. Elizabeth shook her head at her sappiness. From the force of her reaction, you'd think he'd written her a Shakespearean sonnet instead of a few relatively impersonal words.

But once she started bawling, she couldn't stop. Elizabeth teetered back over to her bed and just let the sobs come. Everything that had been festering inside her came spilling out—her disappointment in Finn, her anger at the way he'd treated her, the incredible selflessness Sam had shown, the total callousness Todd had treated her to, her complete and total exhaustion from a night of nonrest. By the time her crying had subsided, Elizabeth had no idea how much time had passed, but when she sucked in a dry, deep, ragged breath and let it out slowly, she felt much, *much* better.

She felt cleansed.

Elizabeth sniffled and stared down at the journal and pencil she held clutched in her lap. Since when had Sam become so thoughtful? Not only had he left her this gift, but he'd been totally unobtrusive for the past couple of days. He'd stayed out of her way so that she could have time to think. So she could have some space.

I always knew he was a good guy deep down, Elizabeth thought, gazing across the room at the attic window.

"Deep, *deep* down," she allowed, making herself laugh. Laughing felt even better than crying.

Elizabeth hoisted her exhausted body off her bed and walked over to her cushioned window seat. She reached over and pulled open the blinds, letting the early morning sunshine warm her face and send a pleasant tingling sensation over her weary skin. With a deep breath, she opened her new journal and wrote the date across the top of the first page with her silly Bugs Bunny pencil.

A couple of days ago I thought I would never be happy again, Elizabeth wrote. *But a friend told me everything was going to be okay . . . and I'm starting to think he may be right.*

Something hit Nina's face, and she jolted awake, her heart pounding a mile a minute. She blinked rapidly, trying to get her bearings, then realized there was a hand resting on her forehead. Nina's eyebrows scrunched together in confusion until she realized that hand was supposed to be there. Well, it wasn't *supposed* to be on her forehead, but it belonged to Xavier, so it was okay for it to be in her bed.

Nina rolled over carefully and lifted Xavier's wrist. Ever so slowly she moved his arm so that it was resting on his side. Xavier's head twitched, and he rubbed his nose against the pillow, but he didn't wake up. Stifling a giggle, Nina watched him as he slept. He looked so adorable, cuddled up in her light blue sheets with no shirt on. She could just lie around and run her hands over his perfect chest for hours.

A door slammed somewhere on her floor, and Nina sat up.

What time is it? she thought, squinting at the sunlight blaring through the windows. She brought a hand to her forehead. *Wait a minute . . . what* day *is it?*

Nina glanced at her clock. It was twenty after nine. And it was Tuesday, she realized finally. That meant Calc IV started in about half an hour. Ugh! What had ever possessed her to become a physics major? There were just too many heavy classes involved. She should be taking journalism classes like Elizabeth. The girl got to watch *Nightline* and *Entertainment Tonight* as homework.

Gingerly Nina lifted back her covers and slid out of bed. Xavier didn't move a muscle. He stayed in his half-diagonal position, as if he were still leaning up against her body. In a moment of sheer dorkiness Nina leaned over and tucked the blankets around him. There was no point in waking him up. Xavier had scheduled nothing but afternoon classes for himself so that he could always sleep in.

"Smart guy," Nina whispered, tiptoeing over to her underwear drawer. She pulled on a clean pair of panties and a bra, then headed for her closet.

"Whaddaya doin'?"

Xavier's unexpected words froze Nina in place. She turned and smiled at him.

"Getting ready for class," she said, pulling a T-shirt off a plastic hanger.

Xavier propped himself up on one elbow and reached his other arm out toward the foot of the bed, where Nina was standing. "Oh, no, you don't," he said, flicking his fingers to beckon her toward him.

Nina pursed her lips jokingly. "What am I, your servant woman?" she asked, putting her hands on her hips.

A wide grin spread across Xavier's face, making Nina's heart flutter like a moth. "Maybe you are," he said. Before Nina could even move a muscle, Xavier lunged for the end of the bed and grabbed her wrist.

Nina squealed as he pulled her back down with him, cradling her in his arms. "You're not going anywhere," he said with a grin. He brought his lips to hers and kissed her deeply. Nina lost herself for a moment, letting him run his rough fingertips down her bare arms.

Finally she pulled back. "I have to go," she said, rubbing her nose against his.

"Nope," Xavier said. "If you're my slave, you have to do what I tell you. And I'm ordering you to stay."

He brought his lips toward hers again, but Nina ducked away at the last minute and, taking him by surprise, managed to roll out of his arms. She stood up and pushed her hair back from her face.

"Educated servants are more valuable anyway," she said, pulling on her T-shirt. "Just imagine what I'll be worth to you when I'm a calculus expert."

"C'mon, Nina," Xavier said, patting her pillow and looking up at her with puppy-dog eyes. "Don't leave me here all alone." He reached out and took her hand. Against her conscience's will, Nina inched closer to the bed, never taking her eyes from Xavier's. She sat down as he brought her palm to his face and kissed it gently. "I'll make it worth your while," he said in his deep, baritone voice.

Nina closed her eyes as he trailed kisses up her arm. "Besides," he said, pausing for just a moment. "I bet you already know calculus forward and backward."

She didn't even realize she was leaning toward him until she felt his mouth softly caressing her neck.

Okay, she thought as her brain went foggy with pleasure. *The boy does have a point.* She *was* the person all her classmates came to with questions, and she never even needed to consult the book to answer them.

What was skipping one little class going to hurt?

Elizabeth had always loved the smell of books, but she especially loved the smell of the SVU bookstore. It was the crisp, almost plasticky smell of new textbooks, mixed with the warm scent of new fleece clothing. It always took her back to her first day of freshman year when she'd walked in all psyched to learn and start her new life. As she roamed the aisles, Elizabeth shook her head and smiled. She'd been through a lot since then, but she'd always remember that excited feeling she'd had.

Nothing that had happened in the past year could take that away from her.

Elizabeth paused in front of a big crate of notebooks that were on sale, two for the price of one. She was about to grab a couple of spirals when she saw a familiar shock of blond hair emerging from the specialty-book room at the back of the store.

Finn. Elizabeth turned, ready to duck behind a coffee-mug display and pray that he would pass her by, but it was too late. He'd seen her see him, and he was on his way over.

Suddenly Elizabeth was very, *very* absorbed in the crucial choice between a red notebook and a white notebook.

Finn walked up right next to her, his jacket brushing her arm. Hadn't he ever heard of the concept of personal space? Her heart was pounding so swiftly and loudly, she was sure he could hear it.

"Nice work, Elizabeth," Finn said. "Setting your attack dogs on me, I mean."

Elizabeth looked up at him, baffled. "What?" she asked.

"Very mature," Finn said, picking up a notebook, glancing at it, and then replacing it on the stack. He leaned toward her. "What did you do? Give Sam a new set of baseball cards to get him to attack me?"

"*Attack* you?" Elizabeth said, facing him fully now. "What are you talking about?"

Finn eyed her for a moment, as if trying to decide if she was sincere. "I can't believe you don't know," he said finally. He chuckled and shook his head. "If you didn't tell him to do it, I at least assumed he'd be bragging about it all over the place. The idiot dumped an *entire* cup of hot coffee in my lap yesterday at the Red Lion."

Elizabeth's jaw hit the floor. There were no words to express what she wanted to say at that moment. She was part stunned, part elated, part horrified, and part jealous—that she hadn't thought to do it herself.

"He *did?*" she blurted out. It came out gleefully, so she supposed that was the emotion that won out.

Finn's cheeks flared up as he stared Elizabeth down. "Yeah," he said harshly. "And the loser's lucky I'm not suing." He crossed his arms over his chest and rolled back his shoulders. "He probably thinks he's a big tough guy now," he said in a teasing voice. "But he just made an idiot out of himself."

Elizabeth looked up at the cocky expression on Finn's face, and suddenly she felt the bile start to rise up in her throat.

"How *dare* you call me and my friends immature?" she spat.

"Oh, here we go," Finn said with a laugh.

Frustration overtook Elizabeth like a wave. She pushed her hands into her hair, holding her bangs back from her face. The anger she felt at that moment was so all-encompassing, she felt as if it were going to start bubbling out of her pores.

"All Sam was doing was defending me," she said, a pocket of emotion almost choking off her words. "It's called *chivalry,* not immaturity."

"Right, Liz," he said. "You're so—"

"Save it," Elizabeth said, disgusted. She had turned on her heel and was about to leave when she realized there was one more thing she had to say to Finn, just for the sake of closure.

"By the way," she said, walking right up to him and tilting her head to the side. She adopted a serious expression. "They say that men who sleep around are usually trying to prove something." She looked him up and down and let her eyes rest on his belt. "You know, compensating for certain . . . inadequacies."

Elizabeth glanced up at Finn's face and smiled slowly when she noticed his ears were bright red. A sign of total, complete embarrassment.

Perfect, she thought. This was a moment that merited immediate recording in her new journal. The moment when Finn Robinson was, at last, rendered speechless.

She sauntered out of the store, finally feeling she could leave Finn behind.

Chapter Five

A few hours later, Elizabeth felt like she was having a minor breakdown, and the other pedestrians in the Sweet Valley Mall probably thought so too. After her confrontation with Finn, just the idea of going home and trying to study made her stir-crazy. She had some aggression to work off, but she hadn't been able to figure out where to go to do it. Somehow the Jeep had found its way to the mall, and Elizabeth had realized it was as good a place as any to power walk.

That was how her mall visit had started out anyway—speed walking through the main concourse and earning frustrated snarls from the people she cut off or obliviously stepped on. But once the anger had worked itself out a little, Elizabeth had started thinking about the other surprise she'd had that day—the fact that Sam had stood up for her.

That thought turned Elizabeth into a meandering, daydreaming window-shopper. Involuntary smiles kept pushing their way onto her face, and then she started getting *baffled* looks from everyone around her. They must have thought she was psychotic—smiling one minute, scowling the next.

In one of her daydreamy moments Elizabeth came to a stop in front of Sports Extra, a clothing store that stocked everything from tennis skirts to football jerseys to in-line skates. She stared at her doofy reflection in the front window and tried to imagine the look on Finn's face when Sam had dumped the coffee on him—the look on Sam's face when Finn reacted. Suddenly Elizabeth laughed out loud, then covered her mouth with her hand.

Lunatic, she thought. But it was kind of a good thing. She hadn't laughed out loud in a long time. And, as it always seemed to be lately, she had Sam to thank.

I should get him something, Elizabeth thought, eyeing a Nike display in the window of Sports Extra. Sam had been nothing but giving lately. It was time that Elizabeth gave something back.

She strolled into the store and headed directly for the back, where there was a baseball-cap display that reached to the ceiling. Sam could probably be in *The Guinness Book of World Records* for his baseball-cap collection. He had more hats than

Jessica had shoes, but like Jessica and shoes, he never seemed to feel he had enough.

Elizabeth walked along the display wall, hoping to find one hat Sam didn't have. It wasn't easy. She recognized almost everything she saw. And the ones that didn't seem familiar were totally wrong. Sam only wore the kind of baseball cap that was soft all over and could mold to his head. He'd never be caught dead in the kind that had a big, hard front and stood inches off his forehead.

Color was a problem too. Sam wasn't exactly the type who would walk around in a neon yellow Lakers hat.

Smiling, Elizabeth stopped in front of a shelf of Major League Baseball hats. She hadn't realized until that moment that she knew enough about Sam to know how he preferred his favorite fashion item. For some odd reason, it made her feel close to him, even though Neil and Jessica could have probably made the same observation.

She reached up and took down an LA Dodgers cap, turning it over in her hands. Sam liked baseball, but she wasn't sure which was his favorite team. And he was such a *guy*, he would probably mock her if she bought him a Dodgers cap and it turned out he liked the Giants or something. She'd never live it down. So much for knowing him so well. Elizabeth dropped that hat and sighed. Maybe this wasn't such a good idea.

Ready to give up and buy the guy a Cross pen or something idiotic, Elizabeth turned around and nearly walked into a rack of NFL hats.

Elizabeth grinned and spun the little rack around. They were perfect—each one was khaki colored with the name of the team embroidered in a classy-looking print across the front. And Elizabeth knew exactly which team Sam liked. The New England Patriots. He'd spent the entire fall screaming about them every Sunday night.

When she found the hat, Elizabeth grabbed it and headed directly for the register. It was the perfect present. It was something Sam could and would use, and it showed that she actually cared about him and listened to him.

Just like he'd been doing for her lately.

"Todd, could you take these receipts and put them back in order by their dates?" Rita asked on Tuesday night, pushing a stack of yellow papers away from her. She sounded exasperated and totally wiped. She was sitting at the chipped wooden table in the back room at Frankie's with the monthly log, piles and piles of receipts, and the checkbook open in front of her. Her head was in her hands, and her curly red hair was sticking out in all directions. "I know you're busy, and I wouldn't ask, but I'm losing my mind here," she added.

Todd placed the plastic bin of glasses he was carrying down on the other side of the table. "What's up?" he asked, picking up the receipts and starting to separate them into piles. "Anything I can do?"

Rita sighed and rubbed her eyes. "You have no idea how much just doing what you're doing helps," she said.

Laughing, Todd shook his head. "My five-year-old cousin could put these in order by date," he said.

"That's not what I mean," Rita said seriously. "I just wish everyone who worked for me was as responsible as you are."

Todd glanced up at her to see if she was kidding, but her brown eyes were as plain and open as ever. A light blush spread over his face, and he paused in his sorting. "C'mon," he said. "I just clean up behind the bar."

"Maybe," she said, leaning back in her rickety wooden chair. "But you always come to work on time, and you never complain when I ask you to stay a little late. All I ever hear around here is, 'But I have to do this,' or, 'I have to leave early to do that.' You're a college student, and I never feel like your job doesn't come first."

Must be because I haven't bothered to do my homework in, like, three weeks, Todd thought wryly.

"You have a great work ethic, Todd," Rita said,

rubbing her hands over her face. He blushed even more and looked down at the receipts.

"Thanks," he said. He didn't bother to tell her that that work ethic only applied to his job and not to school, so it wasn't *all* that impressive.

"I just wish I had half as much energy as you do," she added, staring at a random point above Todd's head.

Todd glanced at her warily. Her eyes were droopy and looked very heavy, as if they could slide off her face. Todd hadn't realized how small she was until that moment. Small and stressed. She must be beyond stressed if she was praising the back-bar guy.

Suddenly Rita pulled her eyes from whatever she was staring at and met Todd's gaze. "I have to figure out a way to get more people in here," she said. "I mean, we're doing okay right now, but if business drops off at all, things could get tight. We need to boost business."

Suddenly the marketing paper that Todd had shoved into the back pocket of his jeans on his way out the door felt as if it were conspicuously expanding. He'd ripped the D from the front page, just like Jodi had done with her C yesterday morning. Should he show it to Rita? Would that be stepping over the line? And what if she thought all his ideas were idiotic?

"Are you okay, Todd?" Rita asked, leaning forward and resting her elbows on the table. "You look a little peaked."

"I'm fine," Todd told her. *If she thinks you're such a great worker, why wouldn't she listen to your ideas?* Todd chided himself. She'd probably be happy to get them from anywhere.

Before he could talk himself out of it, Todd leaned left and pulled the paper out of his pocket. "Here," he said, thrusting the pages across the table at Rita. "I wrote it for school, but it might help . . . maybe."

Rita's eyebrows knit together as she glanced over the front page. Her expression started to soften. "You wrote this for school?" she said, glancing up at him. "Todd, that's—"

Before she could finish her sentence, Cathy, one of the bartenders, burst through the back-room door, clutching a large, white envelope.

"Sorry I'm late," she said, flinging off her jacket and barely even looking at Rita. She shoved the envelope under Todd's nose, practically jumping up and down the entire time. Bemused but smiling over her jitters, Todd took the envelope and read the return address. It was from Orange County College.

"Open it," Cathy said, clutching her hands together. "I can't do it."

"Ma'am, yes, ma'am!" Todd said jokingly. He tore open the flap and pulled out a stack of papers. He didn't even have to read the letter, but he did anyway. "Congratulations," he said, looking up at Cathy. "You're in."

Cathy squealed at the top of her lungs, and before

Todd could even take a breath, she'd pulled him out of his chair and thrown her arms around his neck. "It's all because of you," she said, planting a kiss on his cheek. "If you hadn't helped me with my essay, there's no way I would have gotten in."

Todd blushed scarlet. "Well, I don't know about that," he said, hugging her back.

She released him and turned to Rita. "No matter what you do, my friend, keep this guy around," she said, slapping Todd's chest.

Rita grinned, still holding Todd's paper as she looked up at him. "I was planning on it."

Pride welled up in Todd's chest, lightening his mood like a drug. Cathy grabbed her acceptance letter and ran back into the bar. "I'm in!" she screamed. "I'm going to college!"

As the whole bar burst into applause, Todd and Rita laughed, then walked out to join in the celebration. Todd's heart was as light as air.

At Frankie's, it seemed he could do no wrong. It was a whole world away from SVU.

Sam opened the door of the duplex a few inches, stopped before it got to the width where it always squeaked, and slipped into the house. He paused for a moment to make sure there was no stirring—that no one had heard him come in. Silence. He walked cautiously toward his room, treading as lightly as possible. All he had to do was get inside and lock the door behind him before anyone . . . before *Elizabeth* saw or heard him. Not even Elizabeth would disturb him if his door was locked.

A few steps from the door Sam hit a creaky floorboard, and his heart actually skipped nervously. Was that loud enough for people to hear? He shook his head. Great. Now he was going to be constantly nervous in his own house?

"You did it to yourself, buddy," he muttered, reaching for his doorknob.

"Did what to yourself?"

Elizabeth walked out of the kitchen and leaned against the living-room wall.

Damn. He had been almost home free. It was like she was lying in wait, stalking her prey or something. He glanced up at her and, much to his dismay, she was wearing his favorite little red sweater—the one with the short sleeves and the scoop neckline that made her look like Audrey Hepburn.

"Nothing," Sam said, flinging open his door with now sweaty fingers and walking into his bedroom. He dropped his bag and went straight for his desk, hoping she wouldn't follow.

"So, Sam—"

No such luck. She was standing in his doorway now. He didn't look because that was dangerous, but he could feel her there.

"Listen, Liz," Sam said, shuffling through papers on his desk in an effort to make it look like he was a very busy man. He had no idea what half the papers were, but that was beside the point. He didn't want to have a big, sappy thank-you conversation right now. Or ever. "I can't really talk. I'm late for a study group, and I have to find my . . ." He looked around the room, his mind a total void. "My . . ." Elizabeth arched an eyebrow at him. "My *thing*," he said finally.

"Your thing," she repeated, crossing her arms over her chest.

Sam lifted his worn baseball cap off his head, scratched his fingers through his hair, and replaced the hat backward. He picked up his bag again and squared his shoulders. "I have to go."

He headed for the doorway, and Elizabeth turned sideways so he could get by. Maybe she was going to just let him go without saying anything else. Maybe he could get out of here without a scene.

"Okay, well, I just wanted to say thank you for the presents," Elizabeth said as Sam passed her by.

"You're welcome," he answered without stopping, turning, or even slowing down.

"And thanks for what you did with Finn," Elizabeth called after him.

That one made Sam halt, his foot hovering so that he almost toppled when he came to his abrupt stop. He put his hand on the wall to steady himself and looked at Elizabeth. He could tell that his face was red and only hoped that she couldn't see it from where she was standing.

How had she heard about what he'd done to Finn? What was she, psychic or something?

"It was really no big deal," he said. She smiled. It was a big deal to her. Oh God. How had she found out?

"Well, thanks anyway," Elizabeth said. "I'll talk to you later?"

"Yeah, later," Sam said hesitantly. "I really have to go."

And with that, he finally tore his eyes away from her and sprinted out the door.

Elizabeth finished tying the little silver bow on the box that held Sam's gift and leaned back to admire her handiwork. Maybe wrapping his thank-you gift was a little bit over the top, but she didn't care. She was bored, and she'd done all her homework, and she'd always loved wrapping presents. When she was little, she always used to help her father and brother do it on Christmas and birthdays because they were so inept with scissors and tape.

Now all she had to do was make Sam stand still for five seconds so she could give him the gift. She glanced at her clock and frowned. How long did a study group take anyway? Were they memorizing the Constitution?

"Liz?"

Her heart skipped a beat at the sound of a guy's voice, but then she realized it was just Neil.

"What?" she called back.

"Can you come down here and help me a sec?" Neil yelled.

"Yeah!" Elizabeth pushed herself off her bed and jogged downstairs to Neil's room. Whatever he was doing, it had to be more interesting than staring at the clock.

She found him standing in front of his full-length mirror, shirtless, holding up two shirts on hangers in front of him. As always, Elizabeth was struck by how handsome Neil was. With his jet-black hair, bright gray eyes, and perfect abs, he looked like a soap-opera star instead of a college junior. Living with him might have been dangerous if he were even remotely interested in girls.

"What's up?" Elizabeth asked, plopping onto his bed. "Am I here for a fashion show?"

Neil narrowed his eyes at his reflection, then turned to face Elizabeth. "Kinda," he said, holding out a blue button-down shirt. "Which one's better for a date? This one or this one?" He thrust the other shirt forward—green-and-tan flannel with a tiny plaid pattern.

"I need more information," Elizabeth said, leaning back on her elbows. "Are we talking first date or second date or what? And where are you going?"

Jessica sauntered into the room and leaned back against the doorjamb. "He's not going anywhere," she said, before Neil had a chance to answer.

Neil rolled his eyes at Elizabeth. "Yes, I am," he said, without turning to face Jessica. He tossed the blue shirt down on the bed next to Elizabeth and unbuttoned the collar of the green-and-tan one. He walked back over to the mirror and slipped his arms into the shirt, pulling on the collar to straighten the shoulders. "I'm going to the library with Jason."

"Um, does Jason know this is a *date?*" Jessica asked sarcastically, bringing one finger to her chin as if she were pondering something. "Because if he did, I have the distinct feeling he wouldn't show. Why? Because *he's not gay!*"

"Jessica?" Neil said calmly, looking at her in the reflection from his mirror. Jessica raised her eyebrows. "Go away," Neil said.

"Fine. Make a fool out of yourself," Jessica said. Elizabeth was amazed when the girl actually turned on her heel and walked out. It wasn't like Jessica to back down from a confrontation—even one as bizarre as this one seemed to be.

"What's going on?" Elizabeth asked, picking up Neil's discarded shirt and walking over to his closet.

"Oh, we met this guy, Jason, at the party on Saturday night, and he's really cool," Neil said, tucking his shirt into his jeans. "I really like him, but Jessica thinks he's straight."

Elizabeth hung up the shirt and slid the closet door shut. "What makes her think that?"

Neil grunted a laugh. "Think about it," he

said. "Jessica can't imagine the possibility that there would be one guy in the room who wasn't interested in her . . . for whatever reason."

"You have a point," Elizabeth said with a giggle. She picked up a bottle of cologne from Neil's desk and took a whiff. It smelled like cedar mixed with mint. "Here. Wear this," she said, holding out the bottle to him. "And the shirt you've got on looks great."

"Thanks," Neil said, spritzing himself. "So anyway, Jason's in my poli-sci class, so I asked him if he wanted to go to the library and study for our midterm." He put down the cologne and grabbed his hairbrush. "I don't know, but I think he was pretty psyched." With a huge sigh, Neil stared at his reflection. "I don't know," he repeated.

Elizabeth stuffed her hands in her pockets and shuffled toward the door. "Well, good luck," she said with a reassuring smile. "I hope Jessica's wrong."

"Me too," Neil said, returning the smile. "Thanks, Liz."

"No problem." Elizabeth walked out of the room and trudged back up to the attic. As soon as she was there, she flopped onto her bed with a tired groan. Poor Neil. With all the other pressures of a first date, imagine going out and not even knowing if the guy you were with was attracted to your *gender*.

"God, when did relationships get so complicated?" she muttered. Out of habit she glanced at her clock.

And when did study groups start taking four hours?

Chapter Six

"To Cathy and her paralegal program," Todd said, lifting a glass full of sparkling champagne. The rest of the employees who were gathered around the table in the back room all followed suit, lifting their glasses to toast. "May she be there for all of us when we get arrested, as we all inevitably will one day."

Everyone laughed and shouted, "To Cathy!" Todd sipped his champagne and grimaced as the sour taste hit the back of his throat. He'd never liked the taste of the stuff, but it was standard celebration material. Everyone else drank and then broke down into general chatter.

"Hey! Listen up, everyone!" Cathy shouted, quieting the small, jovial crowd. "I want to make another toast," she said, thrusting her glass in the air again. "To Todd, who I couldn't have done it without."

Todd turned the color of cooked beets as everyone shouted his name and drank again. How could the kids at school scoff at him for having an atmosphere like this to hang out in? These people would be there for him faster than any of his old frat brothers would. In fact, his old "brothers" probably didn't even remember who he was at this point.

"All right! All right, enough partying," Rita said, shooing everyone back out into the bar. "Get back out there before Cathy's and Todd's heads swell any larger." Everyone grumbled but followed orders. Todd was following Cathy out the door when he suddenly felt a hand on his arm.

"Todd, can you hang back for a second?" Rita asked.

Cathy shot Todd a quizzical glance that mirrored his own. "I'll be right out," he told her, then let the swinging black door close, muffling the din of the late-evening bar crowd.

"What's up?" Todd asked, wiping his hands on the seat of his black jeans. Rita walked to the opposite side of the table and picked up a pen. She started tapping it against the tabletop at a psychotically rapid rate. Todd watched her warily. This was definitely a sign of nervousness—not a good thing.

"Wait a minute . . . ," he said, gripping the back of the chair in front of him. "You're not . . . firing me, are you?"

Rita laughed, and Todd pulled back his head as if he'd been slapped. "I'm sorry," Rita said. "It's not funny. No, I'm not firing you. Why don't you sit down?"

Todd pulled out the chair and fell onto the seat, still skeptical. He leaned forward and rested his elbows on his knees, looking over at Rita and wishing she would just get whatever it was over with.

"Look, Todd," she said, holding the pen with both hands now, as if she was trying to keep herself from tapping it. "I'm really impressed with your initiative and your dedication, which you already know."

Todd smiled and glanced away. He was never very good at taking praise.

"What I have to ask you is kind of huge, so I want you to take some time to think about it," she said. "I need an assistant manager, and I'm offering you the job."

Todd was so surprised, he almost forgot to listen to her next words. Him? Assistant manager? Of course! Yes! He was in!

"It pays ten-fifty an hour," she continued.

Ten-fifty? I'm in! I'm in!

"And you'd have to work full-time."

I'm in! I'm . . . Wait a minute. Full-time?

"So, let me know by tomorrow if you can," Rita said, looking him directly in the eye. "I know this is a big decision, and like I said, I want you to think about it. But if you don't want it, I have to start interviewing."

"Okay," Todd said, finally finding his voice. "Thanks, Rita."

"Thank *you*," Rita said with a sincere smile. She grabbed a couple of champagne glasses and patted him on the shoulder as she walked past him and out into the bar.

Todd sat there for a few minutes, staring at a dent in the tabletop that was shaped like a crescent moon. He was so excited, part of him wanted to run after Rita right then and tell her yes. He would do it. There was nothing he wanted more.

But he restrained himself. Todd lightly knocked his clasped hands against his lip, deep in thought. Working full-time would mean quitting school entirely. There was no way he could do both. He was having a hard enough time as it was. So the big question was, what was more important to him? Working at a job he was proud of, supporting himself, and being surrounded by people who cared about him . . . or getting an education in something he hated while encountering snobs and egomaniacs all day long?

Hmmm. This decision was going to be *really* hard.

Elizabeth was just slipping into a dream that involved elephants trampling through the medical school when something startled her awake. For a moment she thought she'd just twitched like she often did when she was about to drift off, but then she realized there were noises downstairs. The refrigerator opening and closing. Keys being tossed on the kitchen table. Heavy footsteps trudging through the living room. Sam's footsteps. She could always tell the difference between his and Neil's because Neil walked like a human being.

Before she could even think about how eager she was going to look, Elizabeth hopped out of bed and rushed over to her mirror. She smoothed down her hair, ran her fingers under her eyes to deal with any smudged mascara, and checked her teeth. Then she laughed at herself. It wasn't like she was going to grab Sam and kiss him. He'd probably laugh in her face even if she did have the guts. She was just going to talk to him.

And give him his present. She dropped to her knees and pulled his gift out from under her bed. Then she straightened her T-shirt and boxers and tucked the box under her arm.

Elizabeth opened her door just as she heard the door to Sam's room swing and click closed. She took a deep breath. When Sam's door was shut, it was very intimidating for some reason. Wandering in there was one thing, but she always felt like she was intruding when she knocked on his door.

Whatever, she told herself. Sam was her

housemate. Her *friend,* even. He wouldn't mind her interrupting. Besides, he'd just gotten there. It wasn't like he could possibly be in the middle of something yet.

Elizabeth tiptoed down the stairs. She took one more moment to make sure all her clothes were in the right place and not bunched up or hanging down. Then she walked purposefully up to Sam's door, tossed back her hair, and lifted her hand to knock.

That was when she heard him laugh.

"I know, yeah," she heard him say clearly. "I had a really good time too."

A really good time? Elizabeth took a step back from the door, her bare feet curling into the thick carpeting. A really good time with who? Who was he talking to?

Oh God, she thought, her stomach turning as her fingers pressed into the wrapping paper on his present. Did he have a girl in there?

Elizabeth looked down at the gift in her hands and suddenly felt like a little child. Sure, she'd told herself she was just buying this for him to thank him, but she wasn't self-denying enough not to realize she was also harboring a little crush on the guy. He'd been sympathetic and chivalrous, and he'd even left her a Bugs Bunny pencil. What more could a girl want in a guy?

Unfortunately she'd somehow forgotten that

Sam had less than zero interest in her. And his defending her and trying to cheer her up after she'd been dumped all over didn't change that. He was probably just taking pity on her.

"I know. We should definitely do it again sometime," Sam said.

Before she heard anything else her vivid imagination could read into, Elizabeth darted away, running as quietly as she possibly could back to her room. Once she was safely inside with the door closed, she dropped the box on the floor and kicked it back under her bed, feeling totally and completely stupid.

Her eyes fell on her new journal, which was sitting on her window seat. She stalked over to it, opened it to the next blank page, and started to write.

Maybe everything's not *going to be okay*, she wrote in a big, angry scrawl. *At least not until I grow up and start facing reality.*

She paused, her heart freezing as she looked over what she'd just written. Slowly Elizabeth sank down onto the window seat.

Maybe Finn was right all along. Maybe she was just a naive child.

Nina slipped her big, black sunglasses over her eyes and reached across Xavier's back for her bottled water. It was a perfect southern California morning, and she and Xavier were taking advantage of the sun by lying out in the quad. He'd brought a big, colorful, comfy blanket, and she'd brought chilled water and snacks, and now they were sprawled comfortably on the ground, letting the world pass them by.

Nina had also brought her book bag, which lay untouched near her feet.

Sighing contentedly, Nina shifted her position and rested her head on Xavier's back like a pillow. She took a sip of water and gazed across the lawn at a guy who was juggling apples in an attempt to impress his girlfriend. There were, in fact, couples all over the place, studying together, dozing together. This was a very couple-y thing to do.

"Comfortable?" Xavier asked, glancing over his shoulder at her.

"Yes," she said, smiling up at him.

"That's what I like to hear," Xavier said, laying his head back down.

Nina sighed again. Okay. She'd spent the last forty-eight or so hours with Xavier, nonstop. They'd eaten together several times, they'd slept together. . . . Hell, they'd made her *bed* together. But even so, there was one question burning in the forefront of Nina's mind. Were they or were they not a couple?

"Xavier? Can I ask you a question?"

"You just did," Xavier said with a chuckle.

86

Nina slapped his back. "Very funny." She took a deep breath and twisted the little white cap back onto her water bottle. "Are you . . . I mean, are we . . . I mean, what exactly do you . . . ?"

Suddenly Xavier rolled over and sat up, jarring Nina out of her comfy little position. *Oh, very articulate,* she thought, sitting up Indian style and running her free hand over her hair. She straightened her batik-print skirt so that it covered most of her thighs.

"What exactly do I what?" Xavier asked, sounding defensive.

"Are we, you know, a couple?" she asked, her heart pounding nervously. She started chewing on the inside of her cheek and had to concentrate in order to stop.

Xavier blinked once, then picked up her hand and kissed it.

"We are right now," he said coyly.

Not exactly the answer she was looking for. "I know," she said, laughing to cover her irritation. "But you know what I mean."

"Nina, you know I don't like labels," Xavier said, pressing his thumb into her palm with a massaging motion. It felt very nice. She didn't, in fact, know he didn't like labels until now, but she was still learning about him.

"Okay, but I do . . . like labels," she said, sounding silly even to her own ears.

"Listen to me," he said, taking her other hand and massaging it in the same slow, destressing fashion. He looked directly into her eyes and pulled her ever so slightly closer. "You and I, we're communicating on a metaphysical plane where no words are truly needed."

Huh? Nina thought. She'd known there had to be pitfalls involved in dating philosophy majors. Like speaking in codes.

He dropped her hands, ran his fingers up her arms, and started to massage her shoulders. Nina rolled her eyes closed and let out a little moan, momentarily forgetting her sarcastic inner voice.

"See?" Xavier said, rubbing more deeply. "That's why our physical connection is so perfect. We don't need words. We don't need labels."

Nina took a deep breath and just let herself go. She let herself feel nothing but his hands. Suddenly she knew that even if he didn't want to say it, there was no way he could be like this with someone else. They *did* have a connection.

Any idiot could see that.

It was only nine o'clock in the morning, and Todd was already showered, shaved, fully dressed, and sitting at his desk, crunching numbers. But he wasn't doing homework for his marketing class. He was calculating how much money he could make in a week at Frankie's if he decided to take the job.

He'd only gotten dressed on the outside chance that he suddenly did a 180 and decided to go to class.

It was easy to figure out, actually. A full-time job meant forty hours a week. So Todd just multiplied forty times ten dollars and fifty cents. He hit the buttons on the state-of-the-art scientific calculator his parents had given him when he'd decided to major in business.

Todd blinked when he saw the numbers. "Four hundred and twenty dollars a *week?*" he said incredulously, looking up at his Magic Johnson poster. Unbelievable. He could pay his rent with less than one paycheck. That couldn't be right. "Okay, that's before taxes," Todd reminded himself. He subtracted twenty percent and was still shocked by how much money he'd be coming home with.

He dropped the calculator on his desk and leaned back in his comfortable rolling chair, propping his arms behind his head. Think of everything he could do with that money. He could eat better, he could save up for a new TV and a DVD player, he could . . . fix his car. Buy a motorcycle . . .

"Yes!" Todd said, leaning over and grabbing his phone from the corner of his desk. He fished in his battered wallet for the card for the garage where he'd had the Beemer towed and dialed the number. This was going to feel so good.

"Regal Garage," a gruff voice answered the phone.

"Hi, this is Todd Wilkins. You have my BMW," Todd said, flipping the card over and over between two fingers.

"Oh! The pretty boy with the pretty car and no money," the gruff voice said with a sneer.

Todd felt the blood rise to his face but decided to let the insult roll off. He wanted to stay in his good mood. *Just think about how good your life is about to get,* he told himself. The thought brought a smile to his lips.

"Yeah, well, just do whatever you need to so I can get it back on the road," Todd said. "I've got the money now."

"Good for you, kid," the voice said sarcastically. "You can pick it up tomorrow." The phone was slammed down in Todd's ear with a loud clanging noise.

Todd rolled his eyes and hit the off button. "Nice guy," he muttered, digging into his wallet again for another number. He found the tiny, creased piece of paper and picked up the phone again, dialing quickly.

His heart started fluttering slightly as the phone rang, and when he heard it pick up, he held his breath.

"Hello?"

"May I speak to Jodi, please?" Todd asked. No intake of air needed.

"This is she," the voice said.

Todd let his breath out slowly and silently. He pushed against the floor with his feet, causing his chair to spin around quickly. "Hey, Jodi," he said. "It's Todd."

There was a brief pause, and for one horrifying second Todd thought she might have forgotten who he was. "From marketing class?" he added, sounding like a complete dork.

"I remember you," she said with a laugh in her voice. "I'm sorry, my roommate was just talking to me at the same time and I had to get rid of her. I was hoping you'd call."

Relieved, Todd pushed with his feet again and rolled across the hardwood floor. He was so psyched, he felt as if he were a little kid. "So, are we still on for tomorrow night?" he asked, spinning again.

"I'm there if you are," Jodi said playfully. "Listen, I know we said we'd complain about class, but do you mind if we actually render that topic untouchable?"

Todd grinned. It was actually a topic he never wanted to talk about again. And as it turned out, he wouldn't have to.

"No problem," he said. "I'm sure we'll have a lot of other things to talk about."

"Good," Jodi said. Man, she had a sweet voice. "So, what do you want to do?"

"Dinner," Todd said, standing up and strolling

across his room to his closet. He swung open the door and pulled his best suit out of the back for the first time in months. "And wear your favorite dress because we're definitely going someplace nice."

"Yeah?" Jodi said, sounding intrigued.

"Yeah," Todd confirmed with a smile.

This was going to be the first date of his new, improved life. And he was going to do it in style.

Chapter Seven

Sam sat at his desk on Wednesday night, trying to get through *A Streetcar Named Desire*. He wasn't sure what had possessed him to take a class called The Modern Drama, but at this point he was wishing he'd signed up for Biomed and Ecological Issues. This Tennessee Williams crap was putting him to sleep. Why couldn't everyone just stop whining and deal? It was like watching an extremely slow, extremely morbid soap opera. Only not as good, and there were no hot babes to look at.

He flipped the musty, dog-eared, used volume closed and tossed it over his shoulder. It fluttered down and then hit the floor with an unceremonious thud.

Sometimes he felt like he needed a tutor or something. But that was so pathetic. It wasn't that he didn't *understand* the reading; it was that he didn't *care*. If he could just get excited about drama and literature like Elizabeth did, he wouldn't be having this—

Damn. Why was she always invading his brain?

At that moment Sam heard a thump from what sounded like the third floor. Right where Elizabeth's room was. He looked up and stared at the stucco ceiling as if he could see through it and get a glimpse of whatever Elizabeth was doing. Straightening up her neat-as-a-pin room, reorganizing her bookshelves, maybe getting undressed for bed—

"All righty, then!" Sam pushed himself out of his chair and picked up his portable phone, hitting the speed-dial number for his friend Ricky. He had to do something to distract himself.

"Yo!"

Sam smiled. "Hey, man. What's up?" This was perfect. A nice, long, intelligence-free conversation would do him good.

"Burgeonator!" Ricky replied. "What's going on, dude? How are those scrumdiliumptious twins you're living with?"

Sam gripped the phone. "Fine. So what's going on with you?"

"Not much, man," Ricky replied. "So when are you going to hook me up with that Liz chick? She is a full-on hottie, my friend. We're talking the cheese and the whiz."

If it were physically possible for a person's head to burst free from his neck, Sam would have been decapitated by a wave of disgust.

"I have to go." He hit the off button on the phone before Ricky had a chance to respond, then dropped to the floor on his back and immediately started to do crunches.

Instead of counting, Sam tried to talk himself down each time he pulled his body up.

"Can't . . . let . . . this . . . get to you. Can't . . . let . . . *her* . . . get to you. Don't think about Saturday. Don't think about the smell of her hair. Don't think about . . ."

As Sam worked, the small of his back started to ache from the contact with the floor and his brow started to sweat profusely. But he didn't stop. This felt good. It felt like he was doing something. It felt like he—

Suddenly Sam stopped midcrunch. He'd heard another noise, but this one was closer. He glanced at the ceiling, hoping he'd heard wrong and it had come from up there. Another creak. It hadn't.

It was right outside.

Sam took a long, deep, quiet breath. *She* was right outside. He could smell her apple shampoo from a mile away. After inhaling it for hours on Saturday while comforting her, it was permanently imprinted on his olfactory memory board.

God! Wasn't she ever going to leave him alone?

And what was she doing out there? Hovering? If she wanted something, why didn't she just knock?

Well, then you'd have to open the door, idiot.

As quietly as humanly possible, Sam rose to his feet, coming up an inch at a time, watching the door warily as if it were going to betray him and tell Elizabeth what he was doing. He didn't even straighten his back. He just crawled into his bed, under the covers. Praying his aging box spring wouldn't let out a creak of its own, Sam rolled onto his back, ever so slowly. As his head hit the pillow, there was the softest of knocks at his door.

Sam's heart rate hit warp speed, and he clutched the end of his blanket. Part of him felt so guilty for leaving Elizabeth hanging like this. She probably needed someone to talk to. Just like she had over the weekend. It wasn't like Jessica was ever around, and Sam hadn't seen Nina in days. Maybe they'd had a fight. Maybe she needed to talk about that too. How could he leave her out there?

But when the knock came again, Sam squeezed his eyes shut and pretended to be asleep just in case she decided to open the door. As if Elizabeth ever would. Elizabeth actually respected people's privacy. Elizabeth respected *people*. Period.

Unlike Sam.

He felt as if he were being pressed down into the mattress by a big hunk of shame. But there was nothing he could do. Talking to Elizabeth . . . getting close to Elizabeth . . . was just too dangerous. Before he knew it, he'd be confessing just as much as she had. She'd know everything about him.

And then she'd be too . . . *knowing*. She'd be calling him on every single move he made. And every single move he *didn't* make. Sam knew Elizabeth. And he knew that the more she understood about him, the more she would expect from him.

He would just disappoint her.

And that was one thing Sam definitely could not handle.

"I am one with the couch," Elizabeth muttered, staring blankly at a *Letterman* rerun as she mechanically fed crumbled baked potato chips into her mouth. "The couch and I are but a single entity."

Dave was feeding a baby leopard from a bottle and cracking jokes about how quickly he'd sue if the thing turned on him. Elizabeth was beyond bored.

She closed her eyes, and they stung like she'd just been walking in a wind tunnel. Apparently she hadn't blinked in the hour and a half she'd been catatonic in front of the tube. Elizabeth forced herself up into an almost sitting position, wiping away the tears her eyes had made to save themselves, and groped around for the remote.

Somewhere out there was a life, and Elizabeth really had to get her hands on it.

She found the remote and hit the off button, plunging herself into total darkness. As her watery eyes adjusted, she cast a glance toward Sam's room. Sam was in there, sleeping. At least she thought he was. Maybe she should go knock again.

"Hey, Liz!"

The light was suddenly flicked on, and Elizabeth blinked against the glare. More frustrated tears.

"What are you doing in the dark?" Jessica asked. She looked unbelievably peppy in her bright pink T-shirt. She looked tan and healthy and bright eyed. Elizabeth felt heavy, mopey, and pale.

"Wallowing," Elizabeth said as Jessica plopped down on the bottom step and started to flip through her mail.

"Oh." Jessica tossed a piece of junk mail on the floor. "Is Neil here?"

Elizabeth rolled her eyes and pulled her legs up onto the nubby couch, sitting Indian style. "Hello? I said I was wallowing." She was so sick of being ignored.

Jessica glanced up, a flash of concern in her eyes. "Still Finning it, are we?" she asked.

"Well, I wouldn't put it that way, but there's a lot going on," Elizabeth began, happy to finally have an ear. "You wouldn't believe—"

"I'm sorry, did you say Neil was here or not?" Jessica asked, scanning the cover of a magazine and then tossing it in the junk pile. Elizabeth had the sudden image of herself lying in the heap of discarded mail. Rejected after a quick once-over.

"I don't think so," she answered flatly.

This, of course, got Jessica's attention. She glared at Elizabeth, clutching a Val-Pak envelope. "Well, do you know where he is?"

Elizabeth shrugged.

"Did he leave me a *note?*" The girl was flushing.

Elizabeth shrugged again.

"God!" Jessica exclaimed, standing up and kicking her little pile of paper debris. The Val-Pak was quickly crumpled in her fist. Elizabeth watched as a bright yellow envelope flipped halfway across the room. "I can't believe he hasn't even bothered to tell me what happened between him and Jason last night," she said, hands on hips. "I mean, that's a *huge* thing. And he's my *best* friend. And he doesn't even pay me the common courtesy of being around so we can talk about it?"

Jessica was pacing now, and her perfectly lined blue-green eyes looked like they were going to burst free from her face.

"I know what you mean," Elizabeth said. "I've been trying to pin Sam down for, like, two days, and he just—"

"Ugh!" Jessica groaned, throwing her hands

up in the air. "This is *un*acceptable. When he gets back, he's going to wish he'd never met me." She grabbed her bag and stomped up the stairs, leaving her mess all over the living room and leaving Elizabeth feeling just as tossed.

Elizabeth flopped backward on the couch and closed her eyes. Unreal. Sometimes she wondered if she and Jessica had really once shared a womb or if they were adopted from two totally different families and just *happened* to look alike.

There certainly weren't all that many similarities below the surface lately.

Punching at the little cushion beneath her head, Elizabeth rolled over onto her side. How was it that the only person who'd been there for her since her breakup with Finn was the one person she'd sworn to hate forever just a few months ago?

She let out a long, slow sigh and turned *Letterman* back on. Maybe Sam was just taking a nap and would come out of his room in search of sugar cereal soon.

She really, *really* hoped so.

"Hey, man!" Ryan called out to Todd from behind the DJ booth on Wednesday night. He was back there, chatting it up with two of the waitresses, Annie and Monica. "You look like someone who wants to be asked why he's smiling."

"No reason," Todd lied. He strolled past Ryan's setup, his hands in his pockets, unable to wipe the grin from his face. As he took in the strobe lights, huge speakers, and dry-ice smoke machines, he realized he was seeing everything differently. In a few minutes he wasn't just going to be a back-bar guy anymore. He was going to be in charge of all this—well, sort of.

"Whatever, T.," Ryan said, sorting through shelves and shelves of CDs. "You must be in love or something." He took out a CD, spun it around on his finger, and then popped it into the player. He was already bopping his head to the music before the bass beat even started to pound from the speakers. "You'd better tell me all about it later," Ryan yelled over the din.

"Yeah, Todd," Monica added with a smile, running a hand through her smooth, dark hair. "There are going to be a lot of broken hearts around this place if people start thinking you're taken."

"I'm not taken," Todd said. *Yet,* he added silently, thinking of his date tomorrow night with Jodi. He ran his hand along the top of a monster amp. "Just in a good mood." He turned and walked across the deserted club toward the back room. They would know the cause of his glee soon enough. Cathy was crouched behind the bar, rooting around for something in the cabinet as Todd walked by. He slunk by her, hoping she wouldn't notice. There was no way he could keep this whole thing a secret for five seconds in her presence, and Todd was sure Rita should be the first to know his decision. He quietly pushed through the back doors and held on to them so they wouldn't make a huge noise when they swung shut.

Rita looked up from a glassware catalog she had open on the table in front of her. Her curly red hair was all piled up on top of her head and held there with two pencils and a ballpoint pen. She raised her eyebrows when she saw Todd. His heart was fluttering around nervously.

"So?" she said hopefully.

"I'll take it," Todd answered.

Rita jumped up from her chair, scraping it back noisily against the floor. "Yes!" she said, coming around the table to give Todd a quick hug. "I'm so excited, Todd. Really. You made a great decision."

Todd beamed at her reaction. He knew she wanted him to have the job, or she wouldn't have offered it, but who would have known she'd be so psyched? "I can't wait to get started," Todd said.

"In that case, let's tell everybody," she said, quickly squeezing his hand. Todd had to stifle a chuckle as she retucked her red T-shirt into the belt of her black jeans and pushed a loose curl back from her face, as if she needed to look her best for the announcement. She leaned past him and pushed open the door.

"Cathy!" Rita called out over the music. "Could you ask everyone to come in here, please?"

Todd walked around the table and leaned back against the counter so everyone would have room to crowd in. His nerves were jumping, and the little hairs on his arms were standing on end. This felt so weird. Exciting, but weird. Everything was about to change.

Cathy pushed through the door first, holding it open for the others as she shot Todd a quizzical glance. He blushed and looked away, knowing he was acting totally suspicious. He just wanted to get the news out there already so they could celebrate. Just like they had for Cathy's acceptance letter last night.

"Okay, everybody, I'll get right to the point," Rita said, crossing her arms over her chest and walking over to stand next to Todd. "I've decided to hire an assistant manager, and Todd has agreed to take the job." She reached up and patted Todd on the back, and he finally tore his eyes from the mushed piece of gum on the floor and looked at his friends. He was grinning like an idiot.

Unfortunately they weren't.

Todd's heart dropped as he looked at each of their faces. Cathy's was pale, Ryan's was tight, and the other girls shot each other a surprised glance and then studied the table as if it held a treasure map to the lost city of gold.

Rita cleared her throat. "I think some congratulations are in order," she said in a stern voice that was laced with surprise.

Everyone seemed to shift in place, and then Cathy finally looked Todd in the eye. "Congratulations," she said flatly. Then she turned on the heel of her black high-top sneaker and pushed through the door back into the bar.

Ryan, Monica, and Annie all watched her go, frozen in place as if the room had just been shaken by a brief earthquake and they weren't sure whether it was safe to move.

Ever so slowly Ryan turned his head and glared at Rita. Todd wouldn't have believed it if someone had told him about it, but he *saw* it happen. Ryan was staring her down. Then he finally turned to Todd and stuffed his hands in his pockets. "I'm happy for you, man," he said, sounding anything but. "I have some CDs to put away." He disappeared through the doors.

Todd felt like someone had punched him in the gut. He glanced at Annie and Monica, hoping this was some kind of bizarre nightmare and they were going to be the ones to snap him out of it. No such luck.

"I'd better go put out the candles," Monica said quickly. She cast Todd a quick glance over her shoulder, along with an even quicker smile.

"I'll go with you!" Annie said, as if it were the most exciting proposition ever. The girls disappeared through the doors.

Todd leaned back against the counter again, feeling heavier than a truckload of full kegs. "What the hell was that?" he said, not really expecting an answer.

"I'll talk to them," Rita replied, gripping the back of a chair so hard, her fingertips were white. "I don't know what their problem is, but I'll talk to them anyway." She started for the door, but something inside Todd told him this was his battle. If he wanted his so-called friends to accept him as an authority figure, he was going to have to start here.

"No," he said, stopping Rita in her place. He took a deep breath and rolled back his shoulders. "I'll handle it."

"I am now one with my mattress," Elizabeth muttered, shifting her position for the fifth time in as many seconds. She kicked at her twisted bedsheets furiously and groaned, pressing her palms against her forehead. Her brain was in hyperdrive, flipping through images of Finn on their first date (cutie), Finn on their last date (megajerk), Finn's new girlfriend (mildly pretty), Finn at the bookstore (that one made her smile). But whenever she got to that last snapshot, she just wanted to hit something two seconds later. Because that afternoon when she'd left Finn in the dust, she'd thought she was done with him.

Finn leaning against the wall outside the med school, the sun highlighting his blond hair.

Apparently not.

Elizabeth sat up in bed, giving herself a killer head rush, and whipped the sheets away from her legs. This was it. She'd had enough. She needed someone to vent to, and Sam was the only option. If he wasn't alone, she'd pull him away. If he was asleep, she'd wake him up. If he wasn't here, she'd track him down. *Someone* had to get her out of her own head.

She was out the door and down the stairs without even realizing she was wearing nothing but a skimpy cotton nightgown that just barely covered her underpants. When she reached Sam's door, she pushed her hair behind her ears and leaned in close. She heard faint strains of guitar music and smiled. That probably meant he was up. Sam didn't usually fall asleep with the stereo on.

But wait. Last night she'd heard voices. She wasn't going to let that stop her this time, but she might as well know exactly what kind of scene she was in for. Elizabeth leaned even closer, pressing her ear against the cool, grooved wood.

That was when he opened the door.

Elizabeth lost her balance and fell forward into the room. For a split second she was sure she was about to land on her face, but then something stopped her. Sam. One hand was on her elbow, the other on her shoulder. Her *bare* shoulder.

As she straightened up, Elizabeth changed color faster than a white T-shirt stuck in hot water with a red sock.

"Uh, thanks," she said, looking up into his stunning hazel eyes. Then she glanced down at his fingers, which were still lingering on her shoulder. He snapped away his hands as if he'd been burned.

"No problem," he said, taking a quick step back. He was wearing nothing but a pair of plaid flannel boxers. Elizabeth's pulse was out of control. "You scared me," he added. "I don't normally have people falling into my room."

Elizabeth giggled, and it came out more like a loud guffaw. Her blush deepened. It was time to get this over with, cut her losses, and slink back to her room to obsess. "I just wanted to . . . say thanks again," she lied, pressing her hands together. "For the present and Finn and . . . you know."

She did want to thank him, but what she really wanted was a long heart-to-heart. A big jam session with advice and sympathy and all that great stuff. But she couldn't handle being in his presence for five more seconds. Not when he'd basically caught her spying on him.

She hazarded a glance at his face, and Sam was just watching her. "You don't have to thank me," he said quietly.

Okay, so he didn't think she was a *total* loser. She could tell from his sincere tone. Maybe she could still get out of this with an iota of dignity. With a deep breath, Elizabeth took a step toward him, closing the distance he'd put between them.

She was just going to give him a little thank-you peck on the cheek and say good night. That was mature, right? That was cool.

She quickly leaned in toward his cheek, lips in brief-pucker position, but she did it so fast, she missed her mark. To Elizabeth's sheer, instantaneous mortification, her mouth landed right on top of Sam's—just slightly off center.

Pull away, you idiot! Why aren't you pulling away? her inner voice screamed.

But then Elizabeth realized why. She wasn't pulling away because Sam wasn't pulling away. He had, in fact, placed his hands lightly on her hips. He was returning the pressure of this kiss ever so slightly. Elizabeth's eyes fluttered closed as her heart bubbled with excitement. She was actually kissing Sam.

And then it was over.

Elizabeth opened her eyes and glanced at him. He looked like someone had just zapped him with a stun gun. All Elizabeth knew at that moment was that she had to get the heck out of there before he said anything. Because whatever he said was sure to slice her already battered heart like a Ginsu knife.

"Well, good night," Elizabeth said in a chipper voice that could have come right off the Home Shopping Network. Feeling like the most clueless freak ever to walk the earth, she spun around and fled as fast as her shaky little legs would carry her.

Chapter Eight

"Typical," Xavier spat as he flopped down on the wooden bench that ran the length of Starlights' left wall. "You spend an hour playing until your fingers practically bleed, and they still only give you twenty percent of the cover charge."

Nina moved over slightly to give him some room. Something she'd noticed over the past few days was that when Xavier was angry—even mildly annoyed—he didn't like to be touched. He didn't even like to be breathed on. But before she could put the safety zone between them, he flung his arm around her shoulders and started tapping his hand against the side of her arm.

Nina allowed herself a private smile. If he'd broken his personal-space rule for her, this relationship was definitely progressing.

"Don't think about it that way," Nina said,

touching his chest. "You're getting exposure just by playing here, and you're the featured band tonight." She glanced around the smoke-filled room at the tiny groups of people milling around—talking, downing beers, and laughing in loud, sudden bursts. "Plus you're on your break and no one's split. That's a good sign, right?"

Xavier smiled briefly and glanced at her, tossing his dreadlocks back behind his shoulders. "You're such an optimist."

"Right," Nina scoffed, shifting slightly in her seat. The bench was flattening her butt, and she was pretty sure she had a splinter in the back of her thigh. "I'm an optimist about other people's lives, but not my own."

She looked up at Xavier. He took a long swig of beer and continued to stare at something across the bar. "Xavier?"

"I'm listening," he said. "Not your own. I heard you—I'm just waiting for the Lakers score." He chucked his chin toward the bar, and Nina squinted at the television that hung from the ceiling next to the men's room. How he could hope to read a score on that thing, she had no idea.

"Well, anyway," she continued, playing with the straw in her warming Sprite. "I haven't been doing so well in school lately, and I'm normally a good student."

"Uh-huh," Xavier said.

"I don't mean a regular good student—I'm usually, like, four-point-oh girl," Nina said.

"Right, right," Xavier said.

"And then my friend Liz . . . This guy just basically ripped her heart out and fed it to her for breakfast and I haven't even had a chance to talk to her about it," Nina said, looking up at his profile.

Xavier took another swig of beer and said nothing. Nina felt her stomach twist like a wet towel being rung out. *"Xavier?"* she prodded, sounding like a whiny schoolgirl.

"I *heard* you," he said, staring her in the eye. "Four-point-oh girl. Ripped her heart out." He smirked and planted a quick kiss on her forehead. Nina immediately tensed up. "See?" he added.

Nina reached up, removed his arm from her shoulders, and placed it on the table. Then she turned in her uncomfortable seat and faced him. "Xavier," she said. "About our conversation this morning out on the quad—"

"I have to go help Bones fix that amp," Xavier said, standing abruptly and finishing off his beer. "Hang out for the second set, okay?" He turned around and strode to the stage before Nina even had a chance to nod.

She stared at the empty space where Xavier had been and wondered what the hell had just happened. A glass broke somewhere nearby, and she glanced up, startled out of her stupor. She didn't spot the klutz, but she did notice two guys leaning against the bar across the way, blatantly checking her out. Under their appreciative yet disconcerting gaze, Nina wished she could just crawl under the table and wait out the night. She'd never gotten a second glance from anyone before she started wearing tighter shirts, shorter skirts, and darker nail polish. No one except Bryan anyway, and that hadn't exactly worked out.

One of the guys ventured a smile, and Nina just scowled back. They rolled their eyes at each other and finally turned away, probably searching for their next victim.

Nina squirmed in her seat, pulling down at her miniskirt in an attempt to protect her legs from the splinter-wielding bench. Was this what having a social life was going to be like? Wearing binding and impractical clothes, getting uh-huhed by your so-called boyfriend, having sex, and making no real connections?

As Xavier and his friends started warming up for their second set, Nina was certain of a few things—at that moment she missed her friends, her sweats, and her comfortable desk chair.

Todd woke with a start on Thursday morning and stared blearily at the clock, sunlight practically searing his eyes. Why hadn't his alarm gone off?

What time was it? Which class did he have this morning?

Wait a minute, he thought suddenly. *I don't have class today. Or ever again.* A slow smile spread across his face, and he curled back down into his soft sheets, pulling his comforter up to his chin. He had nothing to do today. Nada. Zilch. Except hang around and wait until it was time for his date tonight. He could get used to this.

Then images of last night flooded his brain, and Todd's smile faded. He'd never had a chance to talk to Cathy or anyone else about the announcement. They hadn't let him. Cathy somehow avoided looking him in the eye all night, and the place had been packed. Todd was so frustrated. He really wanted to know why everyone was so negative about this whole thing. Weren't they friends, or was that all just as fake as all his relationships at SVU?

The phone rang, and Todd groaned. Who would be calling him at this hour? Maybe it was Cathy calling him to tell him why she hated him.

His hand crept out from under the covers. He picked up the receiver on the third ring.

"Hello?"

"You have some *serious* explaining to do, Todd!" The voice was so loud, Todd was sure his eardrum was never going to stop vibrating. He sat up straight in bed, all bleariness instantly gone.

"Dad."

"I just got a call from the bursar's office," his father continued, his voice only getting louder. "They said the most interesting thing to me, Todd."

Todd squeezed his eyes shut. "Dad—"

"They told me that when a student *withdraws* this late in the semester, they can't give even the partial refund," Todd's father continued. "Do you know anyone who's *withdrawn* recently, Todd?"

"Dad, I—"

"How dare you?" his father screamed. "Your mother is hysterical." Todd could actually hear his mom weeping in the background. "She feels like she did something wrong in raising you. How could you throw your life away like this after everything we've done for you? After everything we've *given* you?"

Todd started to see red. He clutched the end of his blanket in a ball with his free hand. Where did his dad get off, trying to tell him what he could and couldn't do just because he was the one with the money?

"I'll pay you back for the tuition," Todd said tightly.

His father actually laughed. "With what?" he spat. "All those tips from the dive where you're slumming?" Todd's mother wailed afresh at this comment.

"Maybe we should talk about this later," Todd said, narrowing his eyes. "When you're calmer."

"Oh, I'm not going to be calmer, Todd," his

114

father shouted. "I am *never* going to be calmer. Not until you march your butt back over to the registrar's office and fix this thing."

Todd tried to take a deep breath, but his chest was so constricted, he could barely manage it. "I'm not going to do that, Dad," he said quietly.

"Oh, yes, you are, Todd," his father said sternly. "Don't bother calling here until you do."

With that, his father slammed down the phone, completely redamaging Todd's ear. Todd slammed down his own phone, even though he knew his father couldn't hear it. He was so angry, he was actually shaking. Todd released his grip on his poor, abused blanket and managed a nice, long breath. He wasn't going to let his father get to him. He had a real job that paid real money. No matter how much they might rant and wail, his parents couldn't tell him what to do anymore.

I'm an adult now, Todd thought, cuddling back under his covers.

More important, he was an adult who could sleep all day!

She put down the mug, and her eyes fluttered closed.

"No," she protested, blinking hard and picking up her pen. "Stay awake." She glared at the problems in her physics book as if they were taunting her. They were, in a way. There was no way she could make sense of velocity and vortices and all that other crap when she was this tired.

You wouldn't be this tired if you hadn't been up all night with Xavier, a little voice said. The voice wanted to make her feel guilty, but all the thought of Xavier did was make her blush. After Starlights they'd come back to her room. Nina was still irritated by all the nonconversations they'd had that day, so she'd just wanted to pass out. No touching allowed.

But all Xavier had to do was run his fingertip down her arm and all was forgiven. She was jelly girl. Nina sighed as her skin tingled at the memory of Xavier's touch. But then her books came back into focus, and she frowned.

In the light of day, everything looked different. This wasn't the kind of relationship she'd always wanted for herself—the kind of relationship she'd always dreamed of. She never knew what Xavier was thinking or feeling, and he wasn't exactly drooling to find out about her inner workings. Nina tapped her pen against the side of her notebook and glanced at the clock. She'd been sitting here in her admittedly cushy desk chair for an hour, and she'd gotten less than nothing done. She knew she wasn't going to be able to concentrate until she talked to Xavier.

Nina reached across her desk and grabbed her

116

portable phone, quickly dialing Xavier's number before she could chicken out. She had to pin him down and ask him where he thought this relationship was going, or she was going to go from four-point-oh girl to academic-probation girl before you could say "scholarship revoked."

There were a few clicks, and then the grating sound of the busy signal assaulted Nina's ear. She clicked off the phone, dialed again, and got the same thing. Odd. She'd thought Xavier's line had call waiting.

Frustrated, Nina tossed the phone onto her bed and looked around her room. Maybe she could find something else to occupy her for a while and then she could come back to physics with a fresh mind.

Her eyes fell on Mr. Ruggles—the teddy bear leaning against the pillows on her freshly made bed. Nina smiled, recalling how Xavier had woken up with the bear curled in his arms this morning. It was so adorable, and when he—

"That's it!" Nina blurted out, pushing back her chair. She couldn't put this off any longer, or she would never get anything done. Once she talked to Xavier, he wouldn't be so omnipresent in her thoughts. She grabbed her denim jacket and her keys and reached for the door. Then on second thought she picked up her book bag, gathered up all the notes, dittos, and textbooks on her desk, and shoved them inside.

No matter how this conversation with Xavier went, Nina figured she would be a lot safer studying in the library. She had to hide out in a place where there were no beds, no bears, and no scent of Xavier's aftershave still hovering in the air.

In the library she'd be safe—as long as she didn't go near any of the men's magazines.

When Elizabeth opened her eyes on Thursday morning, she felt as if she were opening them to a whole new world, a world where she slept solidly and where she slept late, a world in which Finn Robinson didn't matter.

A world in which Sam Burgess was her perfect match.

Elizabeth rolled over and hugged her pillow, smiling as she remembered how mortified she'd been when she'd first come back to her room the night before. She'd clutched this very pillow to her chest protectively and run over that kiss about a million times. Had *she* done it? Had *he* done it? Had he really not pulled away, or was she just delusional? But gradually she'd talked herself down and started to see things clearly.

She and Sam had kissed. And they'd both wanted it to happen. That was blatantly clear.

Elizabeth sat up, grinning like a moron, and stretched her arms out to her sides until her back cracked. It felt so good to feel this free. She took a deep breath of the fresh morning air billowing through her windows.

"How could I have been so stupid?" she asked herself, shaking her head. For the last few weeks she'd done nothing but obsess about Finn—an egotistical, immature, and ultimately cruel guy who wanted nothing to do with her—when all the while Sam was right under her nose.

Sam, who listened to her. Sam, who understood her. Sam, who comforted her. Elizabeth pulled her hair back behind her shoulders and sighed dreamily, remembering the soft feel of Sam's lips against hers. No kiss with Finn had ever felt like that. Sure, she'd been attracted to him—she wasn't in self-denial—but her attraction to Finn had been colored by the fact that she was in awe of him. It made her blush to think it, but she was. He was older and a med student, and he was interested in *her*. There had been a lot of ego and amazement involved.

But with Sam everything was different. Sam really knew her. They even lived in the same house. He knew when she brushed her teeth, he knew how she took her coffee—he even knew that she washed her good underwear in the sink.

Elizabeth chuckled out loud. She and Sam were going to have a perfect relationship because they'd already gotten all the odd revelations out of the way and they still liked each other. How much better could a situation get?

She pushed herself out of bed and padded over to her closet, shoving her feet into her slippers. She grabbed her terry-cloth robe off the hook in her closet and pulled it over her tiny nightgown. As she headed for the door, she caught a glimpse of herself in the mirror and stopped, amazed by what she saw.

She looked happy.

Her face was all flushed, and her eyes were all bright. She looked healthy, almost as if she'd just run a mile but without all the sweat.

Apparently finding the guy she really wanted to be with had a profound effect on her skin tone. The guy she really wanted. Elizabeth couldn't stop smiling. It was just that Sam had turned out to be so perfect. It was like finally, after all this time, they were both in the same place at the same time. In fact, it was perfectly possible that Sam had been obnoxious to her all this time because he had feelings for her and he thought she would never feel the same way.

But she'd always had a soft spot for Sam. She'd thought he was wrong for her, so she'd pushed him away, but now she knew better. She only wished she had seen his true colors sooner—it might have prevented her from ever making her huge Finn mistake.

It was going to be weird, trying to start up a relationship after all the fights and all the tension.

Jessica and Neil were definitely going to think they were loony. But she and Sam could just take the whole thing very slowly. Elizabeth knew that Sam wasn't the type of guy that would ever pressure her into sleeping with him. He was so not Finn.

"He's like the anti-Finn," Elizabeth said with a laugh. All right, enough of this talking to herself. Elizabeth was sure that Sam was just as psyched to see her as she was to see him.

Elizabeth crossed the room in one giant step and rushed down the stairs, pulling the belt of her robe into a tight knot around her waist. Should she just find him, throw her arms around him, and kiss him? She clucked her tongue inside her mouth and grimaced. Yuck. Maybe she should have brushed her teeth.

Sam's door was open, and Elizabeth's heart skipped about ten beats. She slowed her pace so she wouldn't look like a kid on Christmas morning and strolled over to the open door, a serene smile plastered on her face. But there was no point in overthinking her actions so much.

Elizabeth's skipping heart tripped and fell flat on its face. The bed was made, the desk was clear, and the backpack was nowhere in sight.

So much for psyched. Sam was already gone.

Chapter Nine

This time when the phone rang, Todd's hand shot out from under the covers to grab it and instead knocked it completely across the room. Half asleep, Todd popped up his head as his headset skittered along the floor and slammed into his dresser. He crawled out of bed and scurried across the room, grabbing up the phone in both hands.

"Hello?" he croaked out, his eyes half closed. He could barely even remember how he'd ended up on the floor, his back pressed against his open dresser drawer.

"Todd, it's your mother."

He leaned back heavily, slamming the drawer behind him and knocking his head painfully against the dresser. Reaching back, he rubbed furiously at the throbbing pain. His mom never said, "It's your mother." It was always, "It's Mommy,"

123

or "How's my little boy?" Those greetings had irritated the life out of Todd in the past, but this change was disconcerting.

"What's up, Mom?" Todd asked, fearing the worst.

"I'm very angry with you, Todd," she said flatly. At least she wasn't bawling anymore. At least she sounded more rational than his father had.

"I know, Mom," Todd said with a sigh, pulling a rolled sock out from under his butt and flinging it in the direction of his laundry pile. "But Dad didn't let me explain—"

"I just wanted you to know that we're closing your checking account," she said in a matter-of-fact tone, as if she were talking about the tomatoes in the produce section.

"What?" Todd asked, surprised by his mom's nonchalant attitude.

"Your father is at the bank right now, signing the papers," his mother said. "We're not going to bankroll the life of a bum."

There was a long silence, and Todd had to bite his tongue to keep from freaking out. He knew that was what his mother wanted right now. She wanted him to admit that he couldn't live without their money. She wanted him to beg her to put a stop to it. He would go back to school. He would get a business degree.

Well, that wasn't going to happen.

"Okay," he said, as calmly as humanly possible. "Thanks for letting me know so I can cut up my ATM card."

Todd smiled into the next silence. He could practically see the shocked expression on his mother's face as she struggled for a response.

He heard her take a deep breath. "We're also sending someone to pick up the BMW. Your father doesn't see the point in his paying the insurance anymore," she added.

Todd's heart didn't like that one. It started pounding furiously. He'd just dropped a ton of cash to get that thing fixed. He'd used half his own savings. They couldn't just—

"Not a problem," he heard himself say. Where was that calm tone coming from? Was he going schizo? "I can take the bus to work and pretty much anywhere else I have to go. It'll save me the money on gas."

Todd's mother chuckled, and he felt his blood start to boil. She was *laughing* at him now? Did she think he was still five years old and throwing a tantrum because his Big Wheel broke?

"Sometimes I forget how young you really are, Todd," his mother said. "Maybe this will be a good learning experience for you."

Todd felt like crushing the phone in his fist. He got up off the floor and stalked across the room. "You know what, Mom?" he said. "This already has been a good learning experience. I've learned that you and Dad are total . . ." He couldn't say the word he was thinking. Not to his mother. Not even when he was this angry.

Instead he just slammed down the phone, hopefully deafening his mother as his father had him earlier. Todd stood there next to his bed, his hands on his hips, slowly forcing himself to breathe. Everything was going to be fine. He had a full-time job. He still had his own money in the bank. It wasn't much, but it was enough to get him through until the paychecks started rolling in.

He was going to be fine.

He lowered himself onto his bed and clasped his hands in front of him, resting his elbows on his knees. He couldn't believe how passive-aggressive his mother was being. It wasn't like her. She was usually the levelheaded one who always spoke her mind.

Todd's dropping out must have really hurt her. He ran a hand through his brown curls and sighed, guilt washing over him like a cold wind. He hated hurting his mother.

But what about what she just did to you? he reminded himself. God! She was acting like she was possessed or something. And his father had taken time out of his usually busy day to go down to the bank and cut him off. What was *with* these people?

"I'll just save up and buy my own car," Todd

muttered to the empty room. "Then they can kiss my butt." He couldn't wait to prove them wrong.

He lay down again and stared up at the ceiling, telling himself to think about something else. Something happy. His mind immediately focused on his upcoming date with Jodi. She was so damn beautiful in sweats and a baseball cap, he could only imagine what she'd look like all dressed up to go out.

He envisioned himself pulling up to her house and getting out of the car with a huge bouquet of—

Suddenly Todd's breath caught in his throat. Pulling up? Getting out of the car?

What car?

"So they didn't *do* anything, and Jason didn't *say* anything to make him think it, but Neil is still convinced that Jason's gay," Jessica said incredulously, the wind whipping her hair all around her face.

Elizabeth smiled, barely listening, as she drove the Jeep through the back roads outside campus, winding her way back to the duplex. Jessica could rant all she wanted about Neil's possible love life. Elizabeth wouldn't even point out it was none of her sister's business. At that moment she didn't care. Class had gone well—probably because it had flown by due to her extremely vivid Sam daydreams—and now she was on her way back to the house to talk to him. Finally.

She was sure he'd just had an early class she'd forgotten about, and that was why he'd disappeared that morning. But she knew he didn't have class from eleven until at least one. He was always around the house between those hours.

"What are you so smiley about?" Jessica asked, reaching up to hold on to the roll bar as Elizabeth took a turn far too quickly. "And why are you driving like me?" Jessica paused and raised her sunglasses from her eyes, shoving them back into her hair. "Wait a minute! Did you and Finn get back together?"

"Ha!" Elizabeth spat, following it up with actual laughter. "That's a good one, Jess," she said as she pulled the Jeep up in front of the duplex. It was amazing how tightly Jessica was wrapped up in her own little world.

"Whatever," Jessica said, rolling her eyes as she unbuckled her seat belt. Elizabeth killed the engine, and Jessica climbed out of the car, striding to the door without looking back at Elizabeth once. Elizabeth giggled and shook her head. Normally Jessica's indignation would irritate her, especially since Jessica was the one who'd been ignoring *her*. But right now she didn't care.

She checked her watch as she made her way up the front walk. Right about now Sam should be sacked out on the couch, watching *Guiding Light* and swigging from one of Elizabeth's Dr Pepper bottles. The boy was secretly addicted to the soap opera. At least he thought it was a secret, but he never quite changed the channel in time before Elizabeth caught a glimpse of what he was watching. That was why he hadn't scheduled any classes for the late morning. He was that hooked.

Elizabeth pushed open the front door, smiling. She hated soap operas, but in the mood she was in, she might even join Sam.

Tossing her bag on the floor next to the stairs, Elizabeth came around the corner into the living room and found Neil on the couch, watching CNN.

"Hey, Liz," he said, glancing up.

Her face just about fell off her head.

"Nice to see you too," Neil said with a smirk.

"Sorry," Elizabeth said. "I was just . . . sorry."

She turned on her heel, grabbed her bag again, and trudged toward the stairs. She glanced toward Sam's still empty room and climbed the stairs to her attic bedroom. Once inside, she looked around and sighed, her heart heavy as she remembered how happy and optimistic she'd been that morning. The more time that went by without her seeing Sam, the less confident she was that things had actually occurred the way she remembered them last night.

With a sigh Elizabeth leaned down and pulled

Sam's gift out from under her bed. It was a little dented from the bowling act she'd done with it a couple of nights ago, but it wasn't too bad. Cradling the box in her arms, she made her way back downstairs and walked into Sam's room.

She placed the box in the center of his mattress, then pushed it over slightly so that it really was directly in the middle.

"Freak," she said to herself. She crossed her arms over her chest, hugging herself, and looked around his room. It was such a guy room. Plaid comforter. Sports posters. Girlie calendar. Empty soda cans. Yellowed newspapers peeking out from under the bed. Elizabeth crossed to the closet and quickly glanced over the hat collection that was hanging on the inside of the door—the only well-organized part of the entire room. There were all kinds of baseball caps in all stages of wear, from fraying and dingy to fairly new and not quite broken in. There was one very old red-and-blue Patriots cap, but Elizabeth was glad to see there was nothing like the one she'd bought.

Good. She turned and glanced at the gift again. Sam would be sure to find it, and as soon as he opened it, he would come find her.

At least now she knew she'd see him as soon as he got home.

Whenever *that* would be.

*   *   *

Nina strolled down Xavier's street, her heavy bag weighing her down in the hot sun, her heart pounding against her rib cage painfully. She was sweating like a pig.

There was nothing good about this situation right now. She was hot and tired and nervous, all of which combined to make her clammy, irritated, and probably very, very unattractive.

Maybe this wasn't such a good idea—showing up at Xavier's house unannounced. Nina stopped in her tracks two houses down from Xavier's and stared at a palm tree in the front yard, wondering whether or not she should turn back. She knew she'd be calling herself a wuss later if she did, but did she really care if she thought she was a wuss? Really, what did that matter in the grand scheme of things?

Plus Xavier lived with his parents. Maybe she would disturb them. Maybe they'd want to know who she was. And she couldn't exactly tell them she was Xavier's girlfriend. She was, in fact, here to find out if that was true.

Suddenly Nina felt like a huge imbecile. She knew why she was so scared to walk up to that door, and it had nothing to do with the drop-in or the parents. She was worried she wasn't going to get the answer she wanted.

"Any answer is better than not knowing," she told herself. With that, she took a deep breath and rolled back her shoulders. She walked purposefully down the last stretch of sidewalk and started across the front lawn, her feet sinking into the dewy grass.

Good one, she thought. She hadn't even met his parents yet, and here she was, trampling their lawn. Didn't she used to be smart and considerate and brave and independent? What the heck was wrong with her? Nina climbed the steps and was about to reach for the doorbell when she heard the crash of a cymbal falling over, followed by a round of faint laughter.

Her eyebrows knit together. It sounded like the band was in the garage. That was weird. She didn't think they practiced today. She shrugged. Oh, well. Better to walk in on people she knew than to bother Xavier's mom.

Nina walked down the path this time and crossed over to the driveway. The garage door was open, and Nina immediately spotted Bones messing around with the drum set. She was about to open her mouth to yell out to him when she saw something that made her lose all powers of speech.

Sitting—no, sprawling—on the couch against the far wall were Xavier and some very tall, very red-haired girl. They were going at it so intensely, they didn't even notice when Bones spotted Nina and dropped another cymbal.

"Omigod," Nina said, not meaning to say it

out loud. For a second she couldn't move. She'd just been sitting there with Xavier two days ago. Sitting, although not quite sprawling, on the same damn couch.

But even worse than that, she'd had sex with Xavier *last night*. Those very hands that were all over this girl's back right now had been . . . all over Nina just hours ago.

"Uh . . . Zave?" Bones said.

Nina was going to vomit. She really, really was.

"What?" Xavier said, only removing his mouth from the redhead's long enough to say the word.

"You have . . . uh . . . company," Bones said, shooting Nina a sympathetic glance.

Even more vomit inducing. Xavier finally looked up, and he and the redhead both stared at Nina. It took a moment for realization to spread over Xavier's features. But even before he was all the way there, Nina had spun on her heel and raced down the driveway, her heavy backpack slapping painfully against her back as she went.

By the time she got to the corner, she was bawling. All she could think about was his eyes. She had trusted those eyes. She had loved the way they looked at her. But just now, when they'd locked on hers, they'd been surprised, yes. Caught, yes. But they hadn't betrayed a trace of guilt, or of sorrow, or of sympathy. Nothing but blank surprise.

133

Nina kept running, feeling like her heart was crumbling into pieces behind her. She only felt worse when she realized that half her sorrow stemmed from one simple, pathetic fact. . . .

Xavier wasn't even coming after her.

Sam read the same line of dialogue for the tenth time without absorbing it, then dropped his head to the table with a thud.

"Shhh!" scolded the stern-looking girl at the other end of the table. She shot him a look that clearly told him she thought he was invading her study space. She probably spent every beautiful Thursday afternoon in the library, wasting her life away. Sam, however, wasn't used to it.

"Sorry," he whispered back, adding just a twinge of sarcasm. She didn't seem to notice. The flash cards in front of her were apparently too mesmerizing.

Sam sighed heavily and leaned back in his chair. It let out a tired creak, which elicited another glare from his neighbor, but Sam ignored it as he glanced around. So this was the OCC library. The last time he was here before today was freshman orientation, when they'd taught everyone how to use the computer book-locating system. Sam had spent the entire time spitting his gum into the air and catching it in his mouth again—until it hit the librarian in the face.

He looked past the rows and rows of bookshelves at the high windows at the other end of the room. The sky, as always, was a perfect blue. It was probably really warm out there. Unlike this damn library, where they seemed to think everyone came prepared with parkas and fur hats. Sam pulled his sweatshirt off the back of his chair and pulled it on, then he picked up his book again and stared at the same line of dialogue.

"Why the hell am I doing this?" Sam whispered, pressing his eyes closed. When he opened them, he saw a shock of blond hair over by the computers, and his pulse skyrocketed. *Elizabeth,* he thought, even as he realized there was no possible way it was her. There was no reason on earth for her to trek her butt all the way to the OCC library when she had the much larger, much more sophisticated SVU library down the street.

But it did remind him of why he was here on a perfectly beautiful day. Why he was avoiding his house even though he knew he was missing a pivotal episode of *Guiding Light.* He'd run out of the duplex so fast that morning, he hadn't even had time to program the VCR to tape it. And now he'd never know who the real father of Reva's baby was.

Sam pulled off his hat, scratched at his hair, and replaced the hat, blowing out another short sigh. Why was he putting himself through all of this? He was getting up early. Studying. Missing his soap. And why? All because of a little kiss?

But as Sam remembered the soft pressure of Elizabeth's lips, the scent of her hair, the feel of her hips beneath his hands, he knew it wasn't just a little kiss. It was a brain-numbing, heart-arresting experience. He hadn't felt that way since . . .

Well, since the last time he'd kissed Elizabeth over the summer, when they were on their road trip. Right before they decided they should never see each other again.

"Dammit," Sam whispered.

"Shhh!" the pinched-faced girl said again.

Sam glared at her, his eyes flashing. "Get a life," he said.

"Buy a clue," she shot back. "You're in a library."

"Let me ask you something," Sam said, leaning into the table. "Have you ever been kissed really well?"

The girl's freckled face blushed so deeply, Sam was afraid for a moment that she might pop. Then she just buried her face in her book.

Didn't think so, Sam thought, gathering his books and stuffing them into his backpack. He slung his pack over his shoulder and walked quickly through the stacks, heading for that bright blue sky.

He had no idea where he was going, of course. Maybe he could just go and sit on the beach for the rest of the day. Or maybe he could convince the guys in the student center to switch off ESPN for five seconds and tune into CBS so he could see the last couple of minutes of his show.

Sam pushed through the revolving door at the library exit and took a long, deep breath of fresh air, loving the way the sun felt as it warmed him through his thick blue sweatshirt.

Freedom.

He glanced up and down the street, weighing his options. Maybe he could go home and grab his bathing suit.

Nope. That idea had the word *home* in it. There would be no going there. Elizabeth would be home between classes, and there was no way he could risk seeing her. He rubbed his hand across his forehead, unable to believe he even knew her schedule that well. He was already diseased. How could he possibly trust himself in her presence? He'd probably just grab her and kiss her again, which would be all bad. Well, maybe not *all* bad, but . . .

Sam dropped his head forward, defeated, and stared at his sneakers.

Freedom didn't exactly feel the same when you couldn't even go home.

Chapter
Ten

At nineteen years old, Todd would have thought he'd be way past being susceptible to first-date jitters. He knew what he was doing. He knew what topics to talk about and which ones to steer clear of. He knew not to order ribs or spaghetti (too much risk of messiness). But none of this knowledge helped as he made his way to Jodi's house on Thursday evening.

Maybe it was because he was stepping out of an exhaust-spewing bus that smelled like fresh BO instead of pulling up in his phat car.

Todd straightened his jacket collar and shifted the paper-wrapped roses he'd bought to his other hand. After giving the guys who came for his car his best-possible death glare, Todd had spent the rest of the afternoon searching the paper and the phone book for a good restaurant within walking distance of Jodi's off-campus house. He just hoped Jodi was the type who'd be up for a one-on-one stroll on a first date.

Actually, before the first date even started.

As he walked away from the Fifth and MacGregor bus stop, he hoped he'd made the right choice of restaurant. He was going to have a hard enough time explaining away the lack of a car. Hopefully he wouldn't also have to explain away Formica tables and place mats you could draw on.

Todd stopped in front of the mailbox at 15 MacGregor and looked up at the front door. It was a nice, well-kept little house with a couple of pots of flowers on the front porch. It was exactly the kind of house he would have expected Jodi to live in. Sweet, welcoming, and pretty. He cleared his throat, then blew into his hand and sniffed it. Nothing but mint.

Lifting his chin, Todd walked up to the door and knocked confidently. Jodi appeared moments later, looking beautiful in a simple, short black dress. Her hair was pulled up in a bun with little tendrils hanging around her face.

"Hi!" she said, her eyes lighting up when she saw the flowers.

"Hey!" Todd said, holding them out to her. "You look perfect."

Jodi blushed deeply and sniffed the flowers. "Perfect is a bit of an overstatement, but thanks," she said.

"You're welcome," Todd answered.

"Let me just get one of my roommates to put these in water," she said with a heart-stopping smile. She disappeared inside the house, and Todd had a moment to compose himself. The hard part was over—what to say in greeting was definitely the most nerve-racking moment. Already he'd made her blush and smile. All was well.

"You didn't have to do that, you know," Jodi said, walking out onto the porch and closing the door behind her as she shrugged into a black jacket. She adjusted the strap of a delicate purse on her shoulder as she followed Todd toward the driveway.

"Do what?" Todd asked.

"The flowers," Jodi said. "But I'm glad you did."

Suddenly Jodi's steps faltered. Todd glanced back at her, knowing what was coming as she looked confusedly at the driveway.

"That's kinda why I absolutely did have to do the flowers," Todd said sheepishly, putting his hands in the pockets of his freshly pressed slacks. *Please don't let her think I'm a total loser*, he thought.

"How did you get here?" Jodi asked, looking out at the street.

"I took the bus," Todd said with a shrug. Her face registered extreme surprise.

"All the way out here?" she asked.

"Yeah, well, my car broke down," Todd replied. Not a total lie. "And it was kind of important to me that I get here."

Jodi blushed again. Score one more point for Todd Wilkins. He was primed for a save.

"But I picked a restaurant we could walk to," Todd said, swallowing hard as a slight breeze skittered goose bumps down his neck. Jodi pulled her jacket closer around her body. Todd chose to ignore the fact that it might not be warm enough for a longish walk. "Have you ever been to Dominic's?" he asked, hoping against hope that she wouldn't tell him it was the biggest dive this side of town.

Instead her face lit up. Todd's whole body seemed to sigh in relief. "Only once," she said. "They have the most amazing clams there."

"Great," Todd said, tilting his head toward the sidewalk. "So are you up for a walk?"

Jodi hesitated, and for an instant Todd thought her expression might have clouded again. A moment later the smile was back, however. "I totally would, but these shoes are killers," she said, sticking out one foot to display her high-heeled sandals. Very sexy. "The things a girl will do for a first date," Jodi joked.

Todd smiled. "I'm really sorry—"

"It's okay," Jodi said, holding up a hand.

142

"We'll just take my car." As she fished her keys out of the bottom of her purse, Todd had to wonder why she hadn't just mentioned that idea in the first place, but he decided to let it slide. She was probably just surprised that her date had seemed to materialize on her front step out of nowhere.

He crossed to the passenger-side door of the little red Golf and waited for her to pop the lock. So the romantic walk was out, but at least they were on their way.

He was sure the night was only going to get better.

When Sam emerged from the OCC student center after his fifth pickup game of Ping-Pong, he wasn't surprised to find that the sun had gone down. He put both arms through the straps on his backpack and stretched, letting out a huge yawn. This day had turned him into an expert at wasting time.

In the past few hours he'd read three back issues of *Sports Illustrated*, played a fifty-two-minute-long game of pinball, kicked five freshman butts at the tables, and flirted with at least three girls. He'd even gotten some studying done. Not a bad track record.

Sam tilted back his head and, without any kind of internal warning, let out a loud burp.

"Ugh!" exclaimed a rather mousy-looking girl

as she walked by. "What's your problem?"

"That was a good one," Sam responded happily, patting his tummy. But his stomach wasn't actually very pleased with him. Hanging out in the student center all day also meant eating student-center food all day. And all they had was a Wendy's and a pizza place and about ten vending machines. Sam couldn't remember the last time he'd consumed so much grease.

Sam started to shuffle across the courtyard in front of the student center, walking softly to avoid jarring his delicate stomach. What was he going to do next? Sure, it was dark out, but it wasn't late enough for him to go back to the duplex. Elizabeth would be studying or watching *Friends* right about now. There was no way he could go back until she was safely tucked in bed.

Of course, the thought of her all cuddled up under the covers caused Sam's heart to stir, so he pushed away the image as quickly as possible.

He chuckled to himself as he kicked at a stray rock in front of him. After an entire afternoon of avoiding going home, it had become sort of like a game for him. A challenge. Could he go without his soap? Apparently. Could he make it through all his classes without his midafternoon nap? It seemed so. At this point sustaining his homeless streak was almost as important to him as avoiding Elizabeth.

With a tired groan Sam sank down onto a slate

bench at the edge of the courtyard. He looked around briefly and then swung his legs up onto the seat and stretched out, laying his head down. His back settled in happily, and he let out a long breath. Maybe he could sleep here under the stars. Imagine if he went twenty-four hours? Not that he'd never stayed out that long, but he'd never done it pre-meditated unless he was on a trip or something.

Sam put one hand under his head and closed his eyes. He knew that half the pedestrians he heard walking by him were staring at him, but he didn't care. He was actually comfortable. Except for that bump sticking into the small of his back, and the fact that the slate was so cold, he could feel it through his clothes, and the fact that his stomach was moving around so much, it might have been doing a Kentucky reel.

Who was he kidding? He wanted to go home. He wanted his bed. He wanted to whine very badly.

"Burgess?" Sam heard a familiar voice and opened one eye. Sure enough, his friends Floyd and Bugsy were hovering over him, their eyes so bloodshot, Sam could tell they were either way overtired or very stoned. Bugsy was stuffing the better half of a stromboli into his mouth, and a big blob of tomato sauce fell out and landed with a plop on Sam's chest.

"Sorry, man," Bugsy said with a laugh.

Sam sat up and adjusted his baseball cap. "No

problem," he said, letting out another belch.

"Whoa, dude," Floyd said, taking a comical step back. "What have you been eating?"

"Too much, apparently," Sam said.

Bugsy smiled and continuously nodded, his long, blond hair bouncing around his face. "Righteous, man. You got the munchies too?" He took another bite of his 'boli and half the contents—sausage, peppers, onions, and sauce—landed in a pile at Sam's feet. His stomach shifted dangerously. Add nausea to the list of things he was enduring all because Elizabeth had to go and kiss him out of nowhere.

"We're on our way to Frankie's to shoot some pool," Floyd said, slapping Sam on the back. "You wanna join?"

"I don't know, guys," Sam said, closing his eyes for a second so he could concentrate on not throwing up. The thought of a smoky bar with lots of dancing and sweat and spilled beer didn't agree with him. "I'm pretty tired."

"Oh, don't wuss out on us, man," Floyd said. "If you come with us, we can clean up. Those townies will never believe we can beat 'em."

That's because we can't, Sam thought. *At least not in the condition we're in.* Still, Frankie's wasn't a bad idea. He enjoyed hanging out there because it was low-key and he almost never bumped into anyone from school or from SVU.

The number-one draw, of course, was that there was no way in hell Elizabeth would ever show up there.

"All right," Sam said, standing up slowly. "I'm in."

Elizabeth almost fell out of her chair when the doorbell rang on Thursday night. She immediately dropped the shirt she was folding and ran down the stairs. All night the place had been as quiet as a tomb. Whoever this was had better be damn entertaining.

She grabbed the door, swung it open, and was actually surprised to see Nina standing there.

"Hey!" Elizabeth exclaimed, grabbing her friend up in a hug. "I feel like I haven't seen you in weeks." Not that long ago a Nina drop-by wasn't such a rare thing, but lately they'd both been busy with . . . other things.

"Hi," Nina croaked, hugging Elizabeth back lightly.

"What's wrong?" Elizabeth asked, pulling back. Nina was usually a world-class bear hugger. When she got a good look at her friend's face, Elizabeth realized Nina had been crying. Plus she looked like she'd been half asleep when she'd gotten dressed. She was wearing a rumpled SVU sweater over a black miniskirt and knee-high boots. Definitely not the put-together Nina who Elizabeth knew. She grabbed Nina by the end of her sleeve and pulled her inside, closing the door behind them.

"Nina?" Elizabeth prodded, placing her hand on Nina's back.

"I'm such an idiot, Liz!" Nina said, stomping into the living room and flopping onto the couch. She stretched out as if she were at a psychiatrist's office. "You should just throw me out right now before I rub off on you."

If you only knew, Elizabeth thought. Whatever Nina had done, Elizabeth was sure they could go toe-to-toe on idiocy at this point.

"What happened?" Elizabeth asked. Nina pulled her legs up toward her chest, and Elizabeth sat cross-legged at the end of the couch.

"Oh, I've just been following this guy around like a mutt, hanging out in crappy bars with him and his stupid friends and being all 'oh, you're the greatest,' and then bringing him home with me, like, every night, and now I find out he's totally fooling around behind my back!" Nina looked up and raised her eyebrows at Elizabeth.

"That's pretty bad," Elizabeth said. She adjusted her position on the couch and leaned forward. "*I* followed an egotistical moron around like a mutt and then *almost* slept with him and then got completely dumped, laughed at, and ridiculed, and now I've spent the last few days just sitting around here waiting for a *different* guy to come home because I, like a moron, have developed yet another crush."

Nina's eyebrows knitted together. "Who are you waiting for?"

"Sam."

"Lie," Nina said.

"Truth," Elizabeth admitted.

There was a moment's pause.

"What the hell happened to us?" Nina said finally, pushing herself up into a sitting position.

Elizabeth laughed. "I don't know, but maybe it's because we haven't been spending enough time together."

Nina nodded slowly and pulled one of the throw pillows to her chest. "You're right. That's it. You're not allowed to leave my presence ever again."

"We keep each other grounded." Smiling, Elizabeth leaned back and nudged Nina's leg with her toe. "So tell me about this guy," she said. "And I'll tell you exactly why he's not worthy of your magnitude of perfection."

Nina let out a long, labored sigh and pushed her hair back from her face. She looked around the room blankly, as if she didn't really know where she was. "You know what?" she said. "I don't want to talk about it." She looked at Elizabeth out of the corner of her eye. "You know what I want to do?"

"Pizza bagels and *My Best Friend's Wedding*?" Elizabeth asked with a smirk.

"You know me so well," Nina answered. They

both stood up in unison and headed for the kitchen. As Elizabeth wrapped her arm around Nina's shoulders and gave her a little squeeze, she knew they'd be gabbing about this loser guy before Julia Roberts even found out Dermot Mulroney was getting hitched.

But Elizabeth couldn't think of any other way she'd rather be spending this evening than helping her friend through her problems and burning the roof of her mouth on microwaved cheese.

And as an added bonus, it would distract her from thinking about Sam, and the fact that the present was still on his bed, and the fact that he hadn't come home once all day, and the fact that he could, possibly, be lying in a hospital somewhere.

Or worse.

That it was quite possible he could be avoiding her.

By the time Nina got back to her dorm room, she was fuming mad. Venting to Elizabeth had only made her realize that she could have avoided this whole Xavier situation if she'd just had her head on straight. Not that she wasn't blaming him as she slammed the heavy wooden door to her room closed. He was totally, utterly at fault for being a backstabbing male slut. But if Nina had been true to herself, she never would have met the dirtbag in the first place.

Nina charged over to her closet and flung open

the door ceremoniously. She was so angry, she could barely see straight as she started to pull clumps of clothes off their hangers at random.

"I can't believe how stupid I am," Nina said, pulling down a shimmery black tank top. She held it up in front of her and then chucked it over her shoulder. "Ugh! How could I have *worn* that?" One by one she ripped clothes out of the closet and added them to the growing pile on the floor. "I was a groupie," she ranted. "A groupie! Nina Harper! National Merit Scholar. Honor student. Phi Beta Kappa shoo-in. A groupie!"

Suddenly Nina felt a soft velvet garment in her hands and froze in place. She was holding a dark burgundy shirt, borrowed permanently from one of her new friends. Her favorite acquisition since she'd changed her style.

The shirt she'd been wearing when she first met Xavier.

Before Nina knew what she was doing, she started to cry. Clutching the shirt in her fist, she lowered herself onto her bed. Xavier had been so sweet that night. Of course she'd been sucked in. He'd looked at her like she was a supermodel— talked to her like she was the only girl in the room. He'd acted like she was fascinating to him.

Nina lay back on her bed, letting the tears slide down the sides of her face and into her ears. Why wasn't she enough? Why didn't he want to be her boyfriend? After the way he'd touched her and held her . . . It still gave her chills, even though she was repulsed by her own weakness. She'd thought she was special to him. How could she have been so wrong?

"Wait a minute," Nina said, sitting up abruptly. She wiped her hand roughly across her face and sniffled. "Listen to yourself. You are not allowed to think like this."

She stood up, tossed the shirt into her trash can without a second glance, and then headed back to her discarded clothes. She crouched down, grabbed a few pieces of clothing off the top of her pile, and started launching them at the garbage can.

"Yes!" she shouted as she tossed a red camisole into the can. "Two points."

She flung a miniskirt, and it caught on the edge of the receptacle, then fell off the side. "Too bad," she said, throwing a cropped sweater. It went right in. "But Harper bounces back," she cheered, laughing at her own silliness. She thrust her arms in the air. "Harper is back!"

Walking back to the closet, Nina prepared for another assault on her wardrobe. But a loud rap on her door stopped her in her tracks. Who was stopping by at a time like this? Nina looked down at the clothes that remained on the floor. Maybe whoever it was wanted some new used clothes.

Nina reached over and pulled open the door,

expecting to find her mousy next-door neighbor, Kaya, ready to tell her to keep it down. Instead she found Xavier standing there, leaning casually against the door frame.

"Hey, baby," he said.

"You have to be kidding me," Nina blurted out, even as her heart fell to the floor so fast, she was sure she could hear a whistle in the air as it dropped.

"C'mon, Nina," Xavier said, his brown eyes all droopy. "Don't be like that."

"Be like what?" Nina spat, clutching the edge of the door. "An actual person with actual emotions?"

Xavier frowned apologetically. "Come out and have a drink with me," he said pleadingly. "I'll make it worth your while."

Nina was so shocked at his audacity, she couldn't even find her voice. Instead she released her grip on the door and kicked it, slamming it so hard, the wall shook, and shutting out his smug little face for good.

For a moment she just stood there, almost scared—hoping he wouldn't knock again. She wasn't sure she'd have the strength to stand up to him again. To keep from caving in to those puppy-dog eyes.

But there was nothing but silence, followed by the ping of the elevator as it arrived on her floor.

Xavier was gone.

Nina sighed and glanced around the room, frustrated by the tears that stung the corners of her eyes, threatening to spill over once again. She shook her head, trying desperately to shake all thoughts of Xavier out along with it.

"You shut the door on him literally and figuratively," she told herself. What better way to get closure than by slamming the door in his face?

So why did she feel worse than she had five minutes ago?

Chapter Eleven

"So I was like, 'Hello? If I *didn't* sleep through this class, I'd be so bored, I'd have to kill myself,'" Jodi said, laughing so hard, she could barely get the words out.

Todd put down his water glass so that he wouldn't spill it while he cracked up. "You did not!" he said, his eyes watering.

"I was half asleep!" Jodi whispered, leaning forward as she noticed that a few diners close by were staring at them. "I didn't know what I was saying."

"What did she do?" Todd whispered back.

Jodi took a long, deep breath that came in shaky. "She told me that after the quality of my last paper, she was sure it would be no great loss to the university if I did disappear."

"You have to be kidding me," Todd said, his eyebrows raised.

"All I know is, we had a TA for the rest of the semester," Jodi said, twirling a forkful of linguine around on her plate. She shrugged as she lifted the fork to her mouth. "I think the woman had a major meltdown. I heard she went on sabbatical or something."

Leaning back in his chair, Todd smiled across the candlelit table at Jodi. Her skin seemed to glow in the soft light of the restaurant. She was absolutely stunning. When they had walked in, every man in the room had turned to check her out, and the waiter had been flirting with her shamelessly all night. Plus she was a great story-teller, and he'd found out she was also pretty ambitious. The car fiasco was all but forgotten.

"So after all that, you still got your internship," Todd said, finally taking a sip of his water.

"Hey, she wrote me the recommendation before the little breakdown of our relationship," Jodi said with a smirk.

Todd chuckled and straightened the napkin in his lap before he leaned his elbows on the white linen tablecloth. "It's cool that you already have an internship when you're only a sophomore," he said.

Jodi lifted one tiny shoulder. "I've always been one of those people who has to stay busy, you know?" she said, looking him directly in the eye. "If I didn't fill every hour of the day doing something . . . you know, meaningful or active or whatever, I'd lose it." She paused and smiled, looking up at the crystal chandelier thoughtfully. "I guess that's why I had to sleep in micro. That was the only time I had to nap."

"I'm the exact opposite," Todd said, his eyes twinkling. "I have this talent for cutting my schedule to the bare minimum in order to optimize sleep time."

Jodi laughed and took a sip of her soda. "So no morning classes for you, huh?"

For a split second Todd hesitated. This was it. The moment of truth. Should he tell her he was a college dropout and risk the SVU shallowness factor coming into play, or should he just act like he was still taking the classes he'd been enrolled in yesterday? Todd studied Jodi for a moment. She was watching him with interest, her head tilted slightly to the side, her chin resting on her hand. She was interested in him—he was sure of it. She deserved the whole story.

Taking a deep breath, Todd decided to bite the bullet. "Actually, I'm working at a bar at night," he said, running a hand through his wavy brown hair. "You might have heard of it . . . Frankie's?"

"Sure!" Jodi said, with a quick nod that sent the curls around her face bouncing. "I've never been, though."

Todd grinned. See? That wasn't so hard.

"So you work there to help pay for your tuition,

or . . ." Jodi let her question trail off as she scooped up another forkful of pasta.

There was a quick jab in Todd's heart as he realized she'd misunderstood him, but there was no going back now. "No, I actually work there full-time," he said. She glanced up with a confused expression. "I dropped all my classes," Todd clarified.

Jodi froze midchew. Todd couldn't help thinking she kind of looked like a cow with a big lump of food in her cheek. He started to sweat. Finally Jodi finished chewing and swallowed with obvious difficulty.

"Wait a minute," she said, laying one hand flat on the table. "You don't go to school anymore?"

Todd felt his face redden. "I was just offered the job," he explained. "And it just really feels like the right thing for me right now."

"Really." She said it flatly, so it wasn't a question. "But Frankie's? It's kind of a dive, no?"

All of a sudden Todd realized his elbows were sore, and he looked down. He was pressing them into the table so hard, the tablecloth was starting to pull in his direction. "It's not a dive," he said, lifting his arms and placing his hands in his lap.

He took a deep breath. So her initial reaction was negative. She was just surprised. After all, she'd been in class with him three days ago. Now he was suddenly a career man. Who could blame her? Todd decided to try to lighten the mood.

"You know what?" he said, with all the enthusiasm he could muster under the disappointing circumstances. "We should go by there after we finish eating."

Jodi flopped back in her chair, her perfect posture a thing of the past. "I don't know," she said skeptically.

"C'mon," Todd said, fixing her with his best puppy-dog eyes. "The people I work with are very cool. I'm sure you'll like them. And we can get drinks on the house . . . maybe do a little dancing." He wiggled his eyebrows at her comically, and a smile broke out on her face. It was all Todd could do to keep from sighing in relief. This night could still be salvaged.

"Okay," Jodi said, sitting up again. "I'm in."

By the time she heard a set of keys jangling at the front door, Elizabeth was so sure she was never going to see Sam again, she didn't even look up when the door opened. Sam had obviously been abducted by aliens, or won a trip to Aruba, or suffered a breakdown and decided to go live off the land.

Heavy footsteps stormed into the living room, where Elizabeth was reading an extremely bad romance novel. She didn't even have to take her eyes off the words to know that her sister was standing in the middle of the room, hands on hips, waiting for Elizabeth to pay attention to her.

"Hey, Jess," Elizabeth said flatly, continuing to read. *Her chest heaved as he stepped even closer, reaching out to touch her—*

Suddenly the book was snatched from her hands, and Elizabeth was staring at a very red face that mirrored her own.

"Jess! I was reading," Elizabeth said.

Jessica tossed the book to the other end of the couch, effectively losing Elizabeth's place for her. "I can see that, Liz," Jessica fumed. "But I need you to help me talk some sense into Neil."

Elizabeth pushed herself up on her elbows and stared at her sister. "Neil? Where's Neil?"

The front door slammed shut, rattling every item hanging on the front wall, from framed pictures to cobwebs.

"There's Neil," Elizabeth muttered. She sat up all the way now, waiting for the storm to hit.

"Jessica," Neil spat, walking into the room. His face wasn't nearly as red as Jessica's, but Elizabeth had never heard that tone before in her life. At least not from Neil Martin.

"Neil!" Jessica said, whirling around to look at him. "You are *not* in love after one little nondate!"

Elizabeth's ears went on alert. "In love?" she said. "Neil, you're in love?"

"I didn't say I was in love," Neil said, focused on Jessica with a total vehemence. "I said I really like the guy and it's been a long time since I've even had a crush, and you would *think* that my best friend would be happy for me."

"Unbelievable!" Jessica said, throwing her arms in the air. She walked across the room, and Neil followed her with his eyes, not moving a muscle aside from the one in his jaw that kept flexing in and out, in and out. "Jason is not gay, and he obviously doesn't know you are either."

"Where have you *been?*" Neil yelled, pushing his hands into his hair and holding them on top of his head, causing his eyes to bug out. Elizabeth couldn't believe this. They sounded like a married couple. "Everyone on this campus knows I'm gay!" Neil shouted. "Or have you forgotten the little matter of my very outed campaign for student-body president?"

"Okay, but not *everyone* pays attention to campus politics," Jessica spat back.

"I can't believe this." Neil rolled his eyes and just looked at the floor, shaking his head. Elizabeth could tell he was ready to really explode, but Jessica, the person who was supposed to know him the best, refused to let it drop.

"Neil, I just don't want you to get hurt," she said in a calmer, yet almost desperate tone. "I'm telling you—Jason was flirting with *me* on Saturday night."

His head popped up, and his eyes were full of what could only be called glory. "Oh, yeah?" Neil asked, crossing his arms over his chest. "Then why

161

did he and I exchange numbers and he didn't even ask for yours?"

Jessica let out a little laugh but then tucked in her chin. She looked from Neil to Elizabeth, who could do nothing but shrug and try to hold back the laughter that was threatening to bubble out of her throat. Jessica glanced back at Neil and narrowed her eyes.

"Fine," she said, striding past him toward the staircase. "Get hurt. Just don't come running to me."

She stalked up the stairs, stomping her foot on every single platform as she went.

"Fine! I won't!" Neil yelled.

"Fine!"

There was a door slam, and Elizabeth looked up at Neil. "Wow," she said, having not a clue what else to do at the moment.

"How, in the name of all that is good and holy, have you lived with that girl for nineteen years?" Neil said.

Elizabeth smiled placidly. "I have an incredibly high tolerance for shrieks and pouting."

Neil let out a sigh and managed to lift the corners of his mouth. "Sorry about the interruption," he said. Then he slowly trudged over to the stairs.

Once he was gone, Elizabeth leaned back on the couch and let out a deep breath. Unreal. One month ago, if someone had told her that Jessica and Neil would be at each other's throats and that she and Sam would be getting along, Elizabeth would never have believed it.

She turned her head and glanced at the clock on the VCR. At least she *thought* she and Sam were getting along.

If the alien ship ever beamed him back down, she could find out for sure.

Nina squelched the little voice in her head that was screaming, "No, you moron! Don't do it!" She checked her reflection in the full-length mirror on the back of her door, pulled down on the miniskirt she'd retrieved from her discard pile, and lifted her chin.

"I've always been a fair person," she told herself, looking her reflection directly in the eye. "I've always prided myself on it. And being fair is all I'm doing now."

She turned and grabbed her beaded black purse before she could see the truth behind her own eyes—that she knew this was a stupid move. Somewhere deep inside, she knew she was setting herself up for a fall. But the voice she was listening to sounded so enthusiastic and so rational as she opened the door and strode out into the musty hall of her dorm.

Maybe Xavier just needed a chance to explain. Maybe there was a perfectly good reason for what had gone down. Could Nina really live with herself, knowing she'd slammed her door in the face of a guy who was just messed in the head? Delusional?

A cheating liar? the voice said.

"Nope," Nina said. "Not listening."

She managed not to listen to the little voice all the way over to Starlights. There had to be a perfectly logical explanation for Xavier's behavior. For the past couple of hours she'd been trying to figure out what that could be and coming up blank. But as she crossed the well-lit campus lawns, it finally hit her.

Maybe that girl was his ex-girlfriend or something. Not that that would make him totally blameless, but if that were the case, Nina could actually understand. She started to swing her purse as she worked out the whole scenario in her mind.

Xavier and this girl, Nina named her Betty— she had no idea why; it just came to her. So Xavier and Betty had just broken up a couple of weeks ago (pure conjecture), and it had been kind of a nasty breakup. They hadn't spoken to each other since, and they'd never gotten that closure that a person needs to move on after a breakup. Nina knew how that felt. Without closure, feelings could linger forever—you'd be wondering what the other person was really thinking, whether the breakup was just one big misunderstanding.

Heck! There could be lingering feelings *with* closure.

But Nina was getting off track. She took a deep breath, looked around, and noticed that a couple of girls were shooting her looks as she approached the line outside Starlights. Was she talking to herself?

Nina blushed. Never mind—back to Betty and Xavier.

So Betty had shown up at the garage that day out of nowhere, looking all perfect in that tight little slut dress she was wearing, and Xavier just couldn't help himself. He had to kiss her one last time. That had to be it. That Nina could sort of understand. Getting sucked back in. It had happened to her plenty of times.

It's happening to you now, the little voice said.

Nina stomped it down and handed the bouncer her school ID. He ignored her and stamped her hand with the Under 21 stamp that told the bartender she couldn't drink.

"Like you really have to show me your ID, Nina," he said. Nina's eyes almost popped out of her head. He knew her name without looking at her card? Had she really been hanging out here that much?

Stunned, she stumbled through the door. The people behind her shoved by, and Nina decided she'd ponder her name recognition at Starlights later. It was time to find Xavier and give him a chance to apologize. To explain. To kiss her neck until his lips fell off.

Nina took a few steps into the room and scanned the crowd. It didn't take her long to find the familiar dreadlocks. And it didn't take long for her face to fall along with all her hopes.

Xavier was sitting in the corner, getting very cozy with another girl. Operative word would be *another*. It wasn't even Betty. He was *triple timing* all of them.

Before he could look up and see her seeing him again—before she could be *not chased* for the second time that day—Nina turned on her heel and fled.

"Thanks, Cathy!" Todd yelled over the pulsating music as he took two bottles of beer from the bar. Cathy just grunted at him, without even looking up.

Just ignore her, Todd told himself. He could deal with Cathy at work tomorrow. Right now he was on a date. He glanced at the end of the bar and found Jodi. She was standing there, surrounded by a bunch of rowdy guys who were watching the game on the TV behind the bar. She waved a hand in front of her face, trying in vain to clear the smoke away from her face.

Todd pushed his way through the three-people-deep crowd around the bar and finally reached Jodi's side. Just as he got there, the guy behind her raised his hand to cheer a score and dumped half his beer down the back of Jodi's leg.

"Hey!" she yelled, jumping up.

"Oh! Uh, sorry," the guy said, laughing as he turned back to the game.

"Oh, that's so disgusting," Jodi said, lifting her calf to inspect the damage. Todd grimaced when he saw she was soaked. "Can we *please* get a booth?" she said, looking up at Todd.

"Sure," he said, stepping back to let her by. "I'm really sorry about that," he said, following her. "You want me to go back and pummel the guy?" he added, hoping to get a laugh.

Instead Jodi stopped in her tracks and groaned.

"What?" Todd asked, almost bumping into her from behind. Then he noticed she was leaning down, trying to untangle her dress from the side of the Foosball table she was walking past. What the—

Finally she tugged at it, and it tore loose. "Great!" Jodi said, stalking ahead. "So much for this dress."

Todd glanced down at the table. There was a big crack in the wood veneer, and her dress had caught on a splinter that was sticking out. Making a mental note to bring some wood glue in tomorrow, Todd elbowed his way over to the table where Jodi had sat down in a huff. He slid in next to her and placed the beers on the table.

"I'm really sorry," Todd said, placing his arm behind her on top of the bench. He seemed to be repeating those same three words a lot this evening. "Is there anything I can do?"

"Yeah," Jodi said, reaching out and taking a swig of her beer. "You can take me home."

Todd felt his forehead break out with a sheen of sweat. How had things gone so wrong so quickly? They'd been having such a good time at the restaurant, and on the drive over here he'd told her all about the cool people who worked at Frankie's, so that by the time they'd arrived, she'd almost seemed psyched to meet them. But now she'd been spilled on, snagged, and even ashed on by some idiot when they first walked in.

"Hey, Ryan!" Todd shouted out, catching a glimpse of his friend as he walked by the table. Ryan scanned the tables, trying to find the source of the voice. This would be perfect. Ryan was always nice to everyone. He would win Jodi over and show her Frankie's wasn't the dive she thought it was. "He's the DJ," Todd explained to Jodi. "He'll play whatever you want."

Todd finally caught Ryan's eye, but then his heart fell as a reluctant look came over Ryan's face. "Can't right now, man," Ryan shouted, on the move again. "Busy night."

"Yeah. Nice talking to you too," Jodi muttered. Todd found himself staring at the table. How could this possibly get any worse?

"You know what, Todd?" Jodi said suddenly, slamming her half-full bottle down on the table. "You don't have to bother leaving with me. I'm done."

Todd didn't even have enough time to process what she was saying before she was up and melding into the crowd.

"Wait!" Todd said, taking off after her. Being a hell of a lot bigger, it was harder for Todd to squeeze through the throng of people. After a ton of effort and a slew of stepped-on feet, he finally caught up to her just outside the door.

"Jodi!" he called, freezing her in her tracks. "What is wrong with you?" Todd spat, not meaning for the words to come out so accusatory.

She turned around, her eyes red from the smoke, her skirt torn and hanging down on one side, her shoe stained and wet, her hair falling out of its bun. "What's *wrong* with me is that I thought I was dating a business major, Todd," she said, her face hard. "Not some bartender."

For a moment she just stood there and looked at him defiantly, as if she was waiting for him to take it all back. To tell her she was right and he should go back to school and he'd see her in class on Monday. But he couldn't do that. There was no going back. And he didn't want to.

"I don't know what to say to you," Todd said flatly.

Jodi laughed. "You don't have to say anything to me ever again."

And with that, she jumped into her car, peeled out of the parking lot, and drove off into the night.

Chapter Twelve

"That was not pretty," Todd mumbled to himself as he plopped down into the booth he and Jodi had vacated just moments earlier. Their beers, of course, had already been lifted. Todd didn't even care. He placed his elbows on the table and leaned forward, resting his head in his hands. So much for that whole honesty-is-the-best-policy crap. Apparently honesty got you ditched in the most public way possible.

"Hey, man."

Todd looked up to find Sam Burgess, looking tired and slightly ill, hovering over the table. "Do you mind?" he asked, gesturing with his beer bottle at the bench opposite Todd. For a moment Todd considered telling him to just go away so he could wallow, but there was no point in that. Jodi, in actuality, had turned out to be unwallow worthy.

"Go ahead," Todd said, sitting up a little straighter. "Knock yourself out."

Sam slid onto the booth and put his beer down in front of him, letting out a long, slow sigh. "So," he said, leaning back in the seat and tossing both arms up onto the top of the bench so he basically took up the whole side of the booth. "Was that your girlfriend who just pulled a drama queen?"

Todd snorted a laugh. "That was a first date," he said, avoiding eye contact.

"No way," Sam said. He laughed out loud, causing an extreme blush to take over Todd's neck and face. He glanced up at Sam, but there was no cruelty there. Only sympathy.

"Here," Sam said, sliding his untouched beer across the table. "You need this more than I do."

Raising his palm, Todd shook his head. "Thanks anyway, man," he said. "I'm just not in the mood."

Sam bent forward, leaning his arms on the water-dotted table. He didn't even seem to notice that his elbow was sitting in a big puddle that had been left by the previous occupant's sweaty glass. "It's not worth it," Sam said cryptically, raising one eyebrow at Todd.

Todd glanced out at the boisterous crowd, the loud rounds of laughter making him cringe. He saw some guy stick his tongue down some girl's throat and returned his attention to Sam.

"What's not worth what?" Todd asked, reaching out to play with the little votive candle on the table. He rotated it around in his hand, watching the melted wax around the wick harden as it got too far from the flame.

"The untimely departure of a female is not worth ruining your night over," Sam said, looking like he'd just conveyed the meaning of life.

A short laugh escaped Todd's throat, and he scratched the back of his head. "Except when the whole night's activities were supposed to revolve around said female," he said. He placed the candle down on the table again and just stared at his hands.

"Nooo, man!" Sam said, drawing out the *o* just long enough to make Todd realize the guy was slightly buzzed. "You got it all wrong! It's all about freedom." He raised his hands and looked around him like he was surveying his domain. "What could be better than this, huh? Two cool guys just hanging out on a party night. No chick feelings to worry about. No whining or questions or complaints. We could dance with any girl in this room, no problem, and just walk away. No strings." Sam flashed a self-satisfied smile. "This is the way it should be."

Todd glanced over at the dance floor and saw a bunch of girls dancing together, all decked out for a night on the town. They all screamed as a new song started up—obviously one of their favorites—and started laughing as they moved to the beat. He half smiled and looked back at Sam. "You do have a point."

After all, that's what the whole living-off-campus thing was about in the beginning—more freedom. And after Dana moved out, he was freer still. Now that he'd quit school, there was no reason to tie himself down with other things. He should be living the high life.

"Always listen to Sam. Sam is wise," Sam said, leaning back again. At that moment Annie walked by. Todd grabbed her wrist and ordered another beer. She gave him a tight smile and then hurried off. At that moment Todd couldn't care less about what his work "friends" thought of him and his new job. He was in the midst of starting his new *life*.

Annie returned with the beer and popped the cap. "There you go," she said with a more genuine smile. She either wasn't capable of keeping up the freeze-out or she was hoping for a tip.

"Thanks," Todd said as she scurried away.

He lifted his bottle and nodded at Sam, who took the cue and lifted his own.

"To freedom?" Sam said.

"To freedom." Todd clinked the neck of his bottle against Sam's, and they both took a long swig of their beers.

As they lowered their bottles, they both let out satisfied sighs and smiled at each other. Then

Todd looked out at the crowd again, telling himself he was ready to party.

Unfortunately, after being ignored by Ryan, ditched by Jodi, and privately humiliated, a party was the last thing Todd felt up for.

"Dude, are you sure we can't come in and hang with the ladies?" Bugsy asked as he heavily placed one foot in front of the other, his eyes half closed.

"Keep it down, man!" Sam whispered. He touched Bugsy's shoulder, and the guy almost fell over, face first. Sam reached out both hands, grabbed him, and steadied him.

"Whoa! Thanks!" Bugsy said, rubbing a hand over his eyes. "I thought I was about to meet the sidewalk face-to-face." He laughed loudly, and Sam slapped his hand over Bugsy's mouth. That was when Floyd walked into them from behind.

"Why did you stop?" Floyd asked, looking confused. Sam rolled his eyes and let out a short, frustrated breath. Sometimes his friends were more of a hassle than a source of entertainment.

"Look around you, guys," Sam said, crossing his arms in front of his chest. Floyd and Bugsy obliged, each looking around so quickly, they made themselves dizzy and lost their balance. This time Sam waited for them to right themselves and then continued. "What do you see?" he asked.

"Darkness," Bugsy said seriously.

"A lawn jockey," Floyd answered, his brow knit as if he couldn't remember why he knew what a lawn jockey was.

"Exactly," Sam said. "It's two o'clock in the morning. This is a *neighborhood*, not a dorm. You have to keep it down." He looked from one totally oblivious face to the other. They looked back at him blankly. "Okay?"

"Okay," they said in unison, nodding as if their heads were on springs.

Sam started walking again, his friends trailing behind. He'd parked his car down the street so that no one . . . so that Elizabeth wouldn't hear him pull up. Floyd and Bugsy had no way of getting home, so his current plan was to grab some stuff, drive them back to their place, and crash for the night. He'd been pretty sure he could do that without making any noise, but when he'd parked the car, Bugsy had suddenly announced that he had to use the bathroom or he was going to explode all over the inside of Sam's car.

So here he was, faced with the dilemma of trying to be superquiet with the two noisiest idiots on the planet in tow. Maybe if he made them use the downstairs bathroom—

"Dude, as soon as we get in there, I'm going straight to that Jessica girl's room, and I'm gonna ask her to marry me," Bugsy said. "I don't care what you say."

Sam whirled on him as they reached the driveway next to the duplex. "That's it," he said. "You guys are not coming inside."

"When did you become such a lame ass?" Floyd asked, leaning back against the twins' Jeep. He let his feet go out from under him slightly and sat down hard on the bumper. "This is college. You're supposed to have fun."

"I'm having the time of my life," Sam said flatly, stuffing his hands in his pockets. "Now, if I take you guys in there, are you going to behave yourselves?" *Wow*, Sam thought. *I never thought I'd hear myself sounding like a kindergarten teacher.* He was usually the one on the receiving end of such warnings and lectures.

Floyd and Bugsy looked at each other, then Floyd shoved himself to his feet and they both held up their right hands, regarding Sam with serious expressions.

"We swear," Bugsy said.

"Scout's honor," Floyd answered.

Then they both cracked up, laughing.

Sam rolled his eyes and turned on his heel. "You guys can pee in the bushes," he said. "I'll be right back."

Floyd and Bugsy jeered after him but didn't follow as he made his way around to the back of the house. Sam almost turned around and shushed them, but he wasn't sure if he'd be able to look himself in the mirror later if he allowed himself to become that lame.

It was tough going in the dark, but Sam made it safely around the bushes at the side of the house and crept toward the back door. Before he was halfway there, though, he saw something that made him freeze in place.

Elizabeth's bedroom light was still on.

Damn.

Sam placed his hands on his hips and looked up at the square of yellow light pouring through the attic window. What the hell was she doing up? The girl had an eight-o'clock class in the morning. She was always complaining about it. An eight-o'clock class on a Friday! And Sam was constantly reminding her that she was the one who set up her schedule.

He let out a frustrated groan. Was she waiting up for him? If she was, this was all going a little bit far. But maybe he was just pumping his own ego too much. Yeah, she was awake at an inordinately late hour, but did it have to have anything to do with him? Maybe she was just cramming for a quiz or something.

"It doesn't matter anyway," Sam muttered, turning and starting back toward his friends in the driveway. Whatever the reason, Elizabeth was awake. That was all that mattered. She was awake, and she would definitely hear him come in. And he just couldn't deal with that right now.

It looked like he'd be borrowing a clean T-shirt from Floyd in the morning.

Sam grimaced at the thought. He had a feeling Floyd didn't know the meaning of the word *clean*.

Nina tried not to make too much noise as she trudged over to one of the big, oak tables in the SVU library's reference room on Friday morning. It was hard not to make noise when trudging, though. And in the mood she was in, a trudge was the only walk she could handle.

Her legs felt like they weighed about a hundred pounds each. Add two fifty-pound arms, a heart about as heavy as a shot put, and a bag full of heavy science textbooks, and Nina was lucky she was going anywhere.

She noisily plopped into a wooden chair, drawing annoyed looks from most of the people nearby. Nina barely noticed. She pulled out her physics text and notebook, laying them out in front of her. They looked unfamiliar to her. When was the last time she'd actually studied physics?

Come on, Nina. Get with the program, she told herself, flipping open her notebook. It was time to get her life back. No more messing around. No more partying. It definitely wasn't worth it. Not if the end result was her feeling like this.

Picking up a pen, Nina straightened up and focused on her notes, hoping to refresh her memory about the last lecture—or at least the last lecture she'd attended. But five minutes later she was gazing at a knot in the wooden surface of the table, her eyes going in and out of focus as she imagined what an idiot she'd looked like when she'd walked into Starlights the night before.

By the time she'd walked through the door, she'd been all smiley and raring to go. What must the people around her have thought when her face hit the floor faster than a lead balloon? God! What if Xavier had seen her, and she just hadn't seen him seeing her? Nina dropped her head into her hands as a now familiar pang of pain gripped her heart.

It wasn't like she was in *love* with Xavier, but she definitely could have been if it had gone on any longer. She'd liked him so much, and she'd been beyond attracted to him. How could she have let this happen to herself? All along she'd been one of *three* girls. Maybe even more, she realized with another heart pang.

Stop, she told herself, straightening up and gazing down determinedly at her notebook. It wasn't worth it. Xavier definitely wasn't worth it. She glanced up for a moment to get a pencil out of her bag so she could do a problem and noticed a very cute guy sitting across the room, staring at her.

Nina immediately looked away. She was not going to go there. It didn't matter how blond his hair was or how blue his eyes appeared to be, even from this distance. Another cute boy was the last thing she needed right now. She needed equations. Order. Definitive answers. It was what she'd always thrived on. None of this uncertainty crap.

Against her better judgment, she glanced up again, and this time cute boy smiled at her. Nina automatically smiled back. She couldn't have controlled her cheek muscles if she tried. His smile was infectious.

Her heart started to pound nervously as the guy pushed back his chair and started in her direction. At least the nervous pounding felt better than the ego-bruised pangs.

What are you thinking? a little voice in her head yelled. *You're here to get your life back together, not to snag another guy.*

Nina quickly looked down at her clothes. She was wearing a fairly low-cut cardigan, buttoned up to the V neck with no T-shirt or anything under it. Because she'd gotten used to wearing it, she'd put on some mascara and dark lipstick this morning. Was he only coming over here because she looked like a potential hookup, or did he actually think she was pretty? Maybe he'd seen her books and was a science major too. Maybe this wasn't just about her party-Nina image.

He was at her side now. Nina looked up, blushed, and smiled.

"Hi," he said, his eyes unmistakably roaming over her figure. Nina felt her stomach churn, but then his gaze turned to her books. "A little early for physics, isn't it?"

"What are you studying?" Nina asked, tossing a

glance at his vacated table. His books looked even more hefty than hers.

"Industrial engineering," he said with a laugh. "You got me."

An engineering major, huh? That was a lot more promising than a philosophy major. More solid. Ordered.

"I'm Nina," she said, extending her hand. "Want to join me over here?"

He took her hand and shook it. "Josh," he said. "And I was hoping you'd ask."

Elizabeth turned off the shower and reached around the curtain for her towel. She had to be nuts, getting up for a shower before her eight-o'clock class. But after her late night, there was no way she'd be awake enough for the lecture if she didn't blast herself with some cold water.

She quickly toweled herself off, wrapped the light yellow towel around her head turban style, and grabbed her terry-cloth robe. As she headed for the foggy mirror, she made a conscious effort not to listen for sounds of life from Sam's room downstairs and pulled her robe tightly around her body.

That morning, when she'd woken up in her window seat, still fully clothed, with her face pressed up against the grooved molding around the window, she'd decided it was time to make a change. No more stalking Sam. It was bad for her health and her self-esteem. They lived in the same house. They were bound to bump into each other sooner or later.

Elizabeth leaned in toward the mirror and wiped a space in the fog with the forearm of her sleeve. Her reflection was slightly disturbing. She lightly touched the purple circles under her eyes, then rubbed at the lines in her right cheek—the ones imprinted there by the grooved window molding. She couldn't go to class like this. Her classmates would think she'd slept on the street.

But it wasn't like she could miss class either. They had a test next week, and the professor was giving a review session today. If Elizabeth wanted to have any hope of passing, she absolutely had to show.

"Whatever," she told herself. Who cared what those people thought of her anyway? She unwrapped her towel turban and quickly worked through the knots in her hair. Then she headed for the door, telling herself not to even look in the direction of Sam's room. He wouldn't be up anyway. Not after the late night he'd had the night before. Elizabeth hadn't fallen asleep until after two, and she'd never heard him come home. The kid would be out until at least noon.

She opened the door and hurried down the stairs, telling herself to just make the left and go into the kitchen. That lasted for about five seconds before she glanced over her shoulder.

Oddly, Sam's door was open. Elizabeth stopped

and turned around. Was he up already, or had he just been so tired, he'd forgotten to close his door when he went to bed? If that was the case, she might as well close it for him. That way Jessica and Neil wouldn't wake him up when they got ready for class and/or had their daily fight.

Elizabeth tiptoed over to Sam's room and reached for the door handle. Then, because she couldn't help herself, she peeked inside. For some reason she had the sudden urge to see Sam all cuddled up and passed out in bed.

Instead she saw her gift. It was still sitting on the comforter and obviously hadn't been moved an inch.

Elizabeth just stood there for a moment, too surprised to move. Sam hadn't come home last night? What could that mean? Her hand gripped the doorknob as her mind flipped through a thousand questions.

He'd been out all day *and* all night? What could he have possibly been doing? And with whom? Elizabeth blushed as the last question materialized in her mind. There was no way Sam had a girlfriend. If he did, she would know.

But then where was he? Her heart clouded with doubt.

What could be so important that it would keep him away from home for twenty-four hours?

Chapter Thirteen

"How's it going there, Todd?" Rita asked, pushing through the door into the back room, a cloud of smoke following her. It was the middle of the Friday-night rush, and Frankie's was mayhem. But instead of clearing away glasses and dumping out disgustingly overflowing ashtrays, Todd was sitting at the back-room table, surrounded by papers and schedules.

This was the life.

"I think it's okay," Todd answered, glancing over his neatly drawn rows and columns. He'd just finished drafting the following week's schedule, and he was pretty sure he'd done a fair job. He'd incorporated all the written requests for days off and written a list of suggested alternates for each night in case someone called in sick. "Do we need more than two waitresses on Monday night?" he asked, watching Rita as she hurried around the room, loading up a couple of trays with clean glasses.

"Yeah," she said, grunting as she lifted the heavy trays. "It's Monday Night Football. We need at least three, if not four."

Todd rolled his eyes closed and sighed. Duh. He glanced at Rita, and his eyebrows knitted. "Do you need help with that?" he asked as she slowly made her way to the door, turning so she could back through.

"No, I'm all right," she said. "You stay here. You have to learn how to do this." She lifted her chin toward the schedule, then disappeared into the noisy bar.

Todd looked over his work and shuffled a few people around so that he'd have full staff for Monday night. He scheduled three girls and figured he'd wait on people if he really needed to. Just because he was an assistant manager now didn't mean he was afraid to get his hands dirty.

Satisfied, he posted the new schedule on the bulletin board and walked out behind the bar.

"Todd!" Cathy said the moment he emerged. Todd was so shocked she was speaking to him, he almost keeled over. "I need change." She didn't even look at him but continued making two drinks at once, spilling as much seltzer on the bar as she got into the glass.

Todd glanced at her in confusion.

"Change!" Cathy spat, obviously exasperated. "From the safe?" She fixed him with an irritated glare. "You do have the combination to the safe, don't you?"

There was no way Todd was going to admit that Rita hadn't entrusted him with the combo yet. Not when it was so obvious that that was exactly what Cathy wanted him to say. Luckily Rita walked by at that moment and patted him on the back.

"I'll get the change, Todd," she said. "Why don't you go ask Ryan if he's playing any of the requests? I hear some grumbling out there."

"Okay," Todd said, making his way through the crowd. Cathy's attitude had thrown him a little, but he had to remember that this was his first night. He didn't know everything yet, and there was no way the whole evening was going to go smoothly. As he shuffled his way across the dance floor, avoiding an elbow here and a head butt there, Todd comforted himself with the fact that he did know the code to get into the cash register and he had his very own set of keys to the front door in his back pocket.

This place was practically his.

As he approached the DJ booth, Monica turned around with a huge grin on her face, giddy over some joke Ryan had just told. Todd smiled back and went to say hello, but the moment she saw him, Monica's face fell and she averted her gaze.

Okay, so maybe the place was practically his, but none of the occupants were talking to him.

As Monica hurried off, Todd felt a pit of foreboding in his stomach. This would be the first time he'd spoken to Ryan since the night before, when he'd dissed Todd and Jodi. And he had to criticize the way the guy was doing his job. This was going to be great fun.

"It's your job now," he muttered to himself. "Don't worry about it."

He took a deep breath and glanced up at Ryan.

"Hey, man!" he called out.

Ryan looked down at him, his eyes still cold but less hard than they'd been the night before. "What's up?" he asked.

"Rita—" Todd stopped himself before he made it sound like he was afraid to do his job. He wasn't going to say, "Rita told me to tell you," even though she had. It would sound like a cop-out.

"Listen," he said loudly so Ryan could hear him over the music. "A few people have complained that you're not playing their requests."

Ryan squared his shoulders and picked up a CD, popping open the jewel case and studying the disk. "Yeah, well, maybe their requests suck."

"So mix them in with some good stuff," Todd said, squinting up as the strobe lights started to sting his eyes. "You know, if you—"

"Hey, man!" Ryan said. "Don't tell me how to

do my job." He snapped the jewel case closed and turned his back on Todd, pulling his headphones over his ears.

Todd sighed and turned around, surveying the dance floor he was about to dive into again. He was going to have to have some conversations with these people once the bar closed tonight.

He had to find out why everyone was so irritated by the fact that he'd been promoted. Because there was no way he was going to last a week with everyone giving him the cold shoulder.

Elizabeth was considering banging her head against the kitchen table in frustration when she heard the front door open. Her heart leaped to her throat, but two seconds later, Jessica came walking into the kitchen, all giddy as a schoolgirl.

"Hey, Liz!" she said, grabbing an apple out of the basket on the kitchen counter. "What's up with you?" she asked, flopping into the chair across from Elizabeth. "You look like death warmed over."

"Thanks a lot," Elizabeth said. She'd tried to take a nap earlier in the day, but every time she'd heard even the smallest noise, she'd jolted awake. "Have you seen Sam lately?" she asked her sister.

Jessica pulled down on her blue tank top, straightening it and flicking a little piece of apple off her stomach. "No, actually," she said, taking a huge bite. "Why? Is something wrong?" she asked through her mouthful of food.

Elizabeth was surprised that Jessica even asked. She'd been so preoccupied lately. "Yeah, there is. He didn't come home all day yesterday or last night, and he still hasn't been back, as far as I can tell."

Jessica knitted her brow and stopped eating for a split second. "How do you know he hasn't been here?" she asked.

Because I've been keeping a constant vigil, Elizabeth thought. "Think about it," she said lightly. "Do you see any used dishes, dirty socks, or empty pizza boxes lying around?"

"Good point," Jessica said, taking another bite. "But Sam has a life, and he's stayed out before. What's the big deal? He probably just crashed at one of his slacker friends'."

Elizabeth wasn't about to tell her sister that the big deal was she'd kissed the guy and he'd completely disappeared. She refused to let herself think he was avoiding her, but she didn't want to get into it right now. "I don't know," Elizabeth said. "It just seems like kind of a long time."

Suddenly the back door opened and slammed, and Neil came storming into the room, his neck and face so red, they stood out in stark contrast against his crisp white shirt. Jessica blinked and lifted her chin as he stalked over to her.

"You asked Jason out on a *date?*" Neil shouted, getting right in Jessica's face.

"And here comes round three," Elizabeth muttered. No one heard her.

"Yeah," Jessica said with a shrug. "I did it for you."

"What?" Neil spat.

"Jessica—," Elizabeth began.

"Look," Jessica said, continuing to munch on her apple as she talked to Elizabeth. As if her best friend weren't shooting invisible daggers at her. "I just wanted to prove to Neil that Jason isn't gay, so I called him up and asked him to go to Starlights with me tonight." She turned her gaze to Neil and stared him straight in the eye. "And Jason said yes."

"So that when *I* called him to ask him out for tonight, he said no," Neil said without skipping a beat. "And he sounded baffled that Jessica hadn't told me they were hanging out tonight, making me look like a total moron."

"You guys?" Elizabeth said. "Has either of you considered the idea of *asking* Jason what his sexual preference is?"

They both whirled on her, eyes blazing. "No!" they shouted in unison.

Elizabeth jumped slightly in her seat. "Well, why not?"

"Because I know he's straight," Jessica said.

"He's gay!" Neil shouted.

Jessica stood up abruptly, scraping her chair back against the linoleum floor. "Why can't you get it through your thick skull that I'm only doing this so that you won't get hurt?" she asked, glaring at Neil.

"I'm *already* hurt!" Neil yelled back. "*You* hurt me by asking out the guy *I* like!"

"That's it!" Jessica said, opening the cabinet under the counter and tossing her apple core into the garbage. She slammed the cabinet hard. "My date tonight will prove me right once and for all."

"No, it won't," Neil said. "Because it's not a date. At least it's not to Jason."

With that, Neil turned on his heel and stormed out of the kitchen. From the sound of his footsteps, Elizabeth could tell he was taking the stairs two at a time.

"I can't take this anymore!" Jessica said. She stormed out of the kitchen too.

Elizabeth stood up and grabbed her purse. She had to get out of this house. She was tense enough from waiting around for Sam all day.

But the tension level in the house had just gotten way beyond bearable.

As Sam turned onto his street, he was trying to come up with a way of getting into his room undetected. Too bad he wasn't Batman. That guy definitely had some gadget for sneaking back into the Bat Cave.

"This is getting old," he muttered, driving along slowly. Maybe it was time to face the music and talk to Elizabeth. At this point, it was either do that or move out.

Just as the duplex came into view, Sam saw Elizabeth tear out the front door and hop into the Jeep. Moments later she peeled out of the driveway and headed off in the other direction, driving like a maniac.

Sam didn't even allow himself to wonder what was wrong. All he could see was an open opportunity to get in and get the hell out.

He hit the gas, swung into the driveway, and practically ran up to the front door. The moment he entered, he heard the sound of muffled bass coming through the ceiling. Neil's I'm-pissed-don't-talk-to-me music. At that moment Sam couldn't care less. For all he knew, Elizabeth might just be running to the store for some milk. He might have less than five minutes to do his thing and bolt.

He ran up to his room, grabbed his duffel bag out of his closet, and tossed a couple of T-shirts inside without even bothering to look at which ones they were. Then he tossed in an extra pair of sneakers and turned to his dresser.

But something caught his eye, and he stopped. There was a present in the middle of his bed. A nicely wrapped, obviously thoughtful present.

Sam's heart squeezed. Elizabeth had bought him a return gift. That had to be it. He walked slowly over to the bed as if he were afraid the thing might explode and sat down gingerly on the bedspread.

The first thing he did was carefully open the tiny card and read.

Dear Sam,
   Thanks so much for being there for me.
It means more than you know.
                                        —Liz

With a heavy sigh Sam put the note aside, trying to keep himself from feeling like the biggest jerk in the world. He ripped open the present and popped the top off the box.

"Wow," he said, lifting out the hat and automatically rolling the bill. No one had given him a Patriots cap since he was in high school. He didn't even know a person could get one in California. She had to have put some thought into this. He stood up and crossed to the mirror, slipping the hat onto his head. It was perfect—soft and just the right understated color. With some breaking in, this could definitely be an everyday hat.

Suddenly he caught a flash of blond hair in the mirror, and his heart tried to escape through his mouth.

"Where have you been?"

Relief washed over Sam. It was just Jessica.

He turned and looked at her. She was standing with major attitude in the doorway.

"Elizabeth has been seriously worried about you," Jessica said. Her face was flushed as if she'd been running—or just yelling a lot. It probably wasn't a good time to make her mad, but that never stopped Sam.

"I stayed over at a friend's," he said. "And when I moved in here, I wasn't expecting to get a couple of mothers on my case all the time."

"Oh, very original," Jessica said, rolling her eyes as she stalked off.

Sam grabbed his bag and shoved the hat inside. He had to get out of here before Jessica registered the fact that he had a half-packed duffel at his feet. He couldn't deal with a case of twenty questions right now.

He yanked open a drawer and grabbed a sweatshirt, then pulled a pair of jeans off his chair. Then he rushed into the bathroom and cleared his shelf of shampoo, shaving cream, and other toiletries into his bag with one sweep of his arm.

Within seconds he was out the door and back in his car, well on his way to freedom.

As Rita locked up the front door after the last of the stragglers left, Todd noticed Cathy duck into the back room. Of anyone who worked at the club, she was the person he most wanted to clear things up with. He looked around the bar. The waitresses were all cleaning up their areas, and Ryan had already left after shutting down the lights and speakers around the DJ booth. Todd saw his chance and headed through the swinging doors into the back room.

Just as he walked inside, Cathy ducked into the stockroom. Todd shuffled over to the wooden door and rapped on it with one knuckle.

Cathy looked behind her, saw him, and turned around again, continuing to search one of the shelves.

"Can I talk to you?" Todd asked, leaning against the door frame. After a long shift he was getting so used to the silent treatment, it barely fazed him anymore.

"You're the boss," Cathy said, noisily tossing a drink tray aside.

"Cathy," Todd blurted out harshly. She stopped searching and finally turned around, one hand on her hip, one knee popped out. The classic defiant stance. "What the hell is wrong with you?" Todd asked.

"What's wrong with me, *Mister* Wilkins, is that I knew Rita was planning on hiring an assistant manager and *I* wanted the job," she snapped, tilting her head just slightly.

"So this is a jealousy thing?" Todd asked incredulously. How immature could she be? And what about the rest of them? Was this just a popularity contest, with everyone taking sides?

Cathy laughed and shook her head, rolling her eyes up at the ceiling as if she were dealing with a four-year-old. "It's not a jealousy thing, Todd," she said. "It's a necessity thing. And a fairness thing." She stormed past him out into the back room and started slamming around in the cabinets. Todd turned and leaned on the other side of the door, watching her and waiting for her to explain.

"I needed that job, Todd," she said, slamming doors and rattling glasses as she ransacked the shelves for who knew what. "I needed the money for tuition. And I've been working here a year and a half. You walk in, and within a month you're suddenly manager material." She slammed a door so hard, something inside shattered. "It's just not fair."

"Todd?"

Cathy and Todd both whirled to look at the door to the bar. Rita was standing there, holding it open. "Could you come out here a minute?" she asked.

Todd threw an apologetic glance at Cathy's back and followed Rita. She walked behind the bar and turned to Todd.

"Listen, you're going to have to talk to Annie about hanging out with her boyfriend during her shift," Rita said, making a random note on a cocktail napkin. Todd groaned audibly, and Rita looked up. "Is that going to be a problem?" she asked.

"No! Of course not," Todd answered. "I'll talk to her before her next shift."

"Good. That's it," Rita said, stuffing the napkin into her pocket and starting to move past Todd.

"Rita, wait a second," Todd said. "Can I ask you something?"

"Sure," Rita said, leaning one hand on the bar.

Todd rubbed his forehead, quickly considering what he was about to say. There was a possibility that he might sound like he didn't think he was fit for his job—or that he didn't want the job, which wasn't the case. But Cathy did have a point. She had been there a lot longer, she did need the job more than some seemingly privileged college kid, and on top of that, she was probably more mature. Todd was kind of curious about Rita's reasoning as well.

"Why did I get promoted instead of Cathy?" he asked finally.

Rita let out a short sigh. "Well, Cathy's a good bartender," she said matter-of-factly. "She's social, which helps bring in business, but she's not the most responsible worker I have."

"Really?" Todd asked.

"Think about it," Rita said, picking up a towel and wiping down the counter. "She's never on time, she's sloppy with the register . . . and she doesn't think big picture like you do."

Todd blushed at the compliment, but he couldn't help thinking that Cathy still had a point. Seniority had to count for something. "Well, maybe she just needs a chance," Todd said, leaning back against the bar.

"A chance at what?" Rita asked warily, stopping midwipe.

"I don't know," he said, his brain in hyperdrive. "I have to think about it." Rita was the one who was always impressed with his ability to think big. Maybe it was time to start using that ability in his new job . . . and maybe to help a friend in the process.

Chapter Fourteen

"I have an idea," Todd said, bursting into the stockroom, where Cathy was now searching the top shelf with the help of a precarious stepladder. She teetered the moment Todd walked in. He lunged and grabbed the sides of the ladder, holding it steady before she could fall.

Cathy held her hand over her heart. "You scared me to death," she said, taking a deep breath.

"Sorry," Todd said, blinking up at her. "You okay?"

"Yeah, I'm fine," Cathy answered. She ran a hand over her shaggy blond hair, then shakily descended the ladder. "What's up?" she asked when she was safely on the floor.

"What if we split the job?" Todd asked, his grin so wide, it hurt his face.

"What?" Cathy asked, narrowing her eyes.

"Think about it," Todd said, glancing over his shoulder to make sure Rita hadn't followed him into the back room. "We each take half the week—working at least one night together to give Rita that night off and make the shifts even. That way we're both still making more money, and on the nights we're not managing, we can help out with the other person's normal duties."

Cathy cracked a smile, but it quickly fell away. "Don't do me any favors," she said.

"It's not that," Todd said as she walked away from the shelves. "I think it would actually be cool to work together."

"Really?" Cathy asked, turning to him with a hopeful expression.

Rita pushed through the doors, and Todd and Cathy both looked over at her, smiling.

"Uh-oh," Rita said, freezing in place. "Why do I feel like I'm in for it?"

Cathy walked over to the table, pulled a chair out for Rita, and then sat down in the chair next to it. Rita eyed the open seat as if it might bite her.

"Sit down," Todd said, joining Cathy at the table. "I have an idea."

Rita slowly lowered herself into the chair and looked at their excited faces. "Lemme guess," she said with a half smirk. "You guys want to split the job."

Todd felt his mouth drop open, and he looked

at Cathy, who was just as dumbstruck. "How did you know?" he asked.

Rita pulled a couple of pencils out of her curly red mane, spilling her hair over her shoulders. Then she ran her hand through it, fluffing it out, and sighed. "I've been working here too long, that's how."

"So what do you think?" Cathy asked, placing her hands with their palms together in front of her mouth, as if she were praying. Rita looked long and hard at Todd until he dropped his gaze. He felt like he'd been silently scolded.

"Okay," Rita said, earning a squeal of happiness and a neck hug from Cathy. Todd felt his chest actually puff out with pride. Already he'd solved a major dilemma. "On a *trial* basis," Rita clarified as Cathy released her. Todd could tell from her tone that she wasn't thrilled with the idea, but he was sure he and Cathy would prove her wrong.

"Tomorrow night you'll both be on," she said, pushing herself out of her chair. "We'll see how it works."

"Thanks, Rita," Cathy said, following her with her eyes.

"Yeah, thanks," Todd echoed, suddenly feeling extremely tired. It had been a long, long night. And now that the freeze-out problem was starting to be solved, he felt like a huge weight had been lifted. Without that weight there, though, his back felt squishy and ready to collapse.

"You guys should both go home," Rita said, walking over to the linen closet. "Monica and I will finish up. You have a long night ahead of you tomorrow." She reached into the slim closet and pulled out a Dustbuster.

"That's where it was!" Cathy blurted out.

Todd picked up his jacket and backpack and headed for the back door. Rita wasn't going to have to tell him to leave twice. "I'll see you guys tomorrow?"

They both nodded and waved as Todd pushed through the back door and headed around the building toward the parking lot. It wasn't until he was around the corner that he remembered that he didn't have his car.

Todd's shoulders collapsed forward as he checked his watch. It was after two, which meant the buses weren't running anymore. Which meant he was going to have to walk the three and a half miles back to his apartment.

As Todd took his first step, his whole body screamed in exhausted protest. Moments ago he'd been proud and psyched about his job. Now all he wanted more than anything else in the world was his bed.

He turned onto the sidewalk and shook his head, heaving a long, deep sigh. "I really hope this job is worth it," he said.

*   *   *

Nina woke up late on Saturday morning and instantly smiled. She had a date with Josh that night. This was the first day of her new life. Again.

But things were going to be different this time. Nina swung her legs over the side of her bed and stretched, feeling very Mary Sunshine. This time she had something in common with the guy. Josh was not only cute, but sweet, smart, and a dedicated student. She'd met him when she was in the middle of an intense physics study session. Sort of. He wasn't expecting a party girl, and he wasn't going to get one. Nina took a deep breath and let it out slowly, as if she was letting Nina the all-nighter out with it. She was putting that phase of her life behind her.

Pushing herself away from her bed, Nina walked over to the window and flung open the curtains, expecting to find a blazing sun to match her new-dawn mood. What she was faced with was a totally overcast sky and the first few raindrops splattering against her windowpane.

"That's fine," Nina said, unwilling to let herself get down. "All the better to study in." The one problem with going to school in southern California was that it was always sunny and beautiful, and Nina was always tempted to just go outside and play. To become a total slacker. She'd given in to that temptation lately, and it had to stop. The rain would help. It was like someone was looking down on her and helping her out.

Nina grabbed her shower caddy—a little plastic bucket filled with soap, shampoo, shower cap, toothbrush, and toothpaste—slipped into her robe, and headed for the showers. She was humming as she stepped into the hall and almost bumped into Lydia Mereen, one of her neighbors on the floor.

"God! Why are you so happy?" Lydia asked, rubbing her forehead.

Nina stopped and looked Lydia up and down. She was wearing a black miniskirt and heels and looked like she'd just walked through a tornado.

"Are you just getting in?" Nina asked incredulously, knowing full well that she'd had a couple of mornings like that recently.

"Yeah," Lydia said, shuffling along. "And I have a headache the size of a football field, so quit humming."

Nina rolled her eyes. "Sorry," she said, backing toward the bathroom. "Feel better!"

Lydia just groaned and continued on toward her room, her eyes half closed. As she pushed through the heavy wooden door into the bathroom, Nina shook her head. She knew exactly how Lydia felt, and she didn't want to feel that way again anytime soon. What was the point of going out and having fun if you were going to be exhausted, hungover, and miserable the next day? Plus there were times when she could barely remember the "big fun" that had happened the night before. What was the point of that?

She reached into one of the shower stalls and turned on the water full blast, then waited outside the curtain for the water to warm up.

Xavier's probably just as hungover right now, she thought, leaning her head back against the cold ceramic tile. Nina wondered who he was waking up with but immediately pushed the thought aside. She didn't care.

Xavier was obviously not for her.

He was way too much of a party animal. And he had women throwing themselves at him all the time—totally pumping his already swelled ego.

"Kind of like you," Nina said, grimacing as she realized she was just one of those many women. Well, not anymore.

As she slipped out of her robe and stepped into the shower, she felt as if she were washing the past few weeks off herself. She was going to take a nice long shower, put on some cuddly sweats, and head for the library. Somehow the thought of drowning in her books while the rain pitter-pattered against the skylights above was the most comforting thought in the world.

Then, after a good long day of playing catch-up in all her classes, she would change into some nice but conservative outfit and go out on her date.

Nina wondered where Josh was planning on taking her. Definitely not out for a beer and some loud music at Starlights. Josh was sweet. She could totally imagine him having a romantic streak too. He'd probably take her out to some nice restaurant for dinner and then walk her home and give her a nice sweet kiss good night.

Sighing happily, Nina tilted her face up under the water and smiled as it trickled down her neck.

There was nothing like starting over.

Todd folded his nine-millionth white T-shirt and placed it on top of the swaying pile. He couldn't believe how many undershirts he owned . . . and how many he *used*. What did he do, unconsciously change his shirt three times a day?

He hoisted his plastic laundry basket and hooked his bottle of detergent on his finger. Making his way back to the elevator was a tricky business, but he managed to do it without dropping a single clean piece of clothing. But by the time he got back to his apartment, the plastic grooves on the basket handles were cutting into his skin. He dropped the basket to the floor to fish his keys out of his pocket, and the pile of T-shirts toppled over onto the almost never vacuumed floor of the hallway.

"Great," Todd muttered, clicking the lock and practically kicking open the door. He gathered up all the shirts and tossed them on top of his other laundry in a bunch. Then he carried the basket into his room and looked around, placing his hands on his hips.

"Unbelievable," Todd said. "This place is spotless." He was actually proud of himself. He'd spent the whole day playing homemaker guy—cleaning his bedroom, washing his sheets and remaking his bed, cleaning out the fridge, vacuuming the whole apartment. He eyed his basket of clothes. He could put them away later.

Right now it was time for a celebratory snack.

Todd crossed the small apartment to the kitchen and pulled open the refrigerator. There was nothing but a bottle of Coke and a bunch of condiments. His earlier excavation had turned up a lot of food—all of which was growing things—and it was now all in the garbage. With an exasperated sigh Todd slammed the refrigerator shut. It looked like he was going to have to add grocery shopping to today's long list of chores.

He picked up his wallet from the table by the door and realized it was curiously thin.

"Damn," Todd said, feeling like a complete idiot. He'd spent all his cash on the date from hell and on the car that he no longer possessed. Todd slapped his hand against the wall in frustration. It would be one thing if he and Jodi had had a good time. Then he wouldn't mind being penniless for a couple of days, but after what had happened, part of him wanted to call her up and demand half the money he'd spent that night back.

Todd laughed at himself and grabbed his keys and a baseball cap to shield him from the rain. It was no big deal. He'd just go down to the bank and get some money out of the ATM machine. Luckily there was a bank just down the block, so he wouldn't have to take some exhaust-filled bus to get there.

Once outside, Todd took off at a jog. It was raining pretty hard, and he was soaked through by the time he got there. He ran over to the ATM machine and ducked under the overhang, happy to have a moment out of the pelting rain. He looked down at himself and realized his T-shirt was clinging to his body like he'd just come out of the ocean. It was practically obscene.

Todd quickly shoved his card into the slot and punched in his security code. Suddenly the machine let out a loud beep, and a message flashed up onto the little blue screen.

"Invalid account?" Todd read aloud. Then his heart turned to stone, and he had to grip the counter underneath the machine to keep from screaming.

His parents had actually closed his account. "They don't waste any time, do they?" he muttered.

He grabbed his card when the machine spit it back out at him and shoved it in his pocket.

Ducking back into the rain, Todd trudged down the street, letting the drops slap against his arms and face. Suddenly he didn't feel like running. He was carless, penniless, and foodless.

What was he supposed to do now?

Elizabeth pulled her favorite blue sweater over her head, fluffed her hair, and stalked out of her room. She was going to talk to Sam, and she was going to do it now. It was eleven-thirty on a Saturday morning. Sam had to be asleep in bed. She was going to march right in there, wake him up, and demand to know why he'd been avoiding the house for the past two days.

She walked over to his door with heavy feet, making as much noise as possible, hoping to rouse him slightly. When she reached the door, she took a deep breath, squared her shoulders, and rapped loudly on the door.

There was, of course, no answer.

"You're going to get up," Elizabeth whispered. "You have no choice." She knocked again, more loudly this time, and waited. Nothing.

"Okay, I'm going in," Elizabeth said wryly. She grasped the doorknob, turned it, and flung open the door.

Sam wasn't there. Elizabeth felt all the pent-up energy flow right out of her. "You have to be kidding me," she said to the empty room. The made bed just stared at her as if it were mocking her. For a moment Elizabeth was really worried. Something really could have happened to Sam. He'd been gone for far too long.

Elizabeth stepped lightly into the room as if she were stepping into a tomb. That was when she realized something was different. Something was missing. The gift.

There was actually a little square indentation in the bedspread where the present had been. Elizabeth touched the cold bedspread and looked around. Sure enough, the crumpled paper and the box lay in the corner as if they'd been kicked there. Elizabeth walked over and picked up the remains. The hat was gone. The note was gone. So either Sam *had* been here or they'd been victim to a burglar who was only after hats.

But when? Elizabeth wondered. When had he come home without her noticing? She'd kept a practically constant vigil for the last twenty-four hours.

Gradually Elizabeth started to notice that a few other things had changed. Sam's suede jacket had disappeared from the back of his chair, and the books that had been strewn all over his desk were gone too.

"On a Saturday?" Elizabeth wondered aloud. This was the most disturbing of developments. If Sam was studying on a Saturday, he'd definitely suffered some sort of brain damage, accompanied by a rare case of trauma to the personality.

Elizabeth's eyes traveled to his closed closet door. Feeling slightly guilty, she walked to the closet, still clutching the remnants of her wrapping job in her hands. She was definitely invading his privacy, but her brain was starting to formulate a suspicion, and she had to know whether she was right.

She grabbed the closet's doorknob and flung it open. Sure enough, Sam's favorite sneakers *and* loafers were gone. A couple of empty hangers stuck out from the rack, as if clothing had been torn off them in a rush. Sam was gone. And he wasn't coming back. At least not for the next couple of days.

Dropping the gift debris on the floor, Elizabeth rushed out of the room and into the kitchen, hoping to find some kind of note letting her know where he'd gone. Maybe there had been some emergency with his family and he'd had to run to the airport.

Elizabeth checked the refrigerator and found nothing but a two-week-old note to call home. Then she checked the counters. There was an unpaid phone bill, a half-eaten bag of pretzels, and a really crusty bowl of something unidentifiable.

No note. Elizabeth felt tears welling up in her eyes as she scanned the room again. How could he do this? How could he just bail and not let his roommates know that he was okay?

She plopped into one of the chairs at the kitchen table and dropped her head onto her crossed arms. And why didn't he even leave a note thanking her for the gift he obviously liked enough to take with him wherever it was he went?

With a loud sniffle Elizabeth lifted her head and told herself to face facts. Sam was avoiding her.

And he was doing a damn good job.

Chapter
Fifteen

Todd stood up as the bus pulled into the stop closest to the SVU bookstore, holding on to one of the handrails. The bus lurched to a jerky halt, and he was thrown forward, then practically fell out the door when it opened seconds later. Todd had to put a hand down on the wet pavement to keep himself from landing on his face. His book bag wasn't so lucky. It swung off his shoulder and splattered into an amazingly deep puddle.

The bus driver laughed.

"Thanks a lot!" Todd shouted as the door hissed closed and the bus took off with a screech of tires.

"Of course, *now* he speeds up," Todd muttered, picking up his backpack and shaking off the excess water. At least the bag was waterproof, so nothing had gotten wet inside. And it had stopped pouring. Todd hoisted the heavy backpack onto his shoulder. A wet patch instantly formed on his side, but he paid no attention. The sky was just sort of spitting now, hitting Todd in the face lightly every few seconds.

Trying not to dwell on the many, many negative aspects of the past few minutes, Todd started across the street. Sure, the bag on his back felt like it was filled with bricks, but soon it would be delightfully empty—for good. In a brilliant flash of genius Todd had realized he did have cash in his possession—practically. He at least had something as good as cash.

He swung open the door to the airy SVU bookstore and strode directly to the nearly deserted counter in the back. One girl sat there, popping her gum, toying with her ponytail, and reading a battered novel. She didn't look up as Todd approached.

"I'd like to sell these books back," Todd announced, tossing his bag onto the counter with a thump. The girl flinched and eyed him with curiosity as he started pulling out his ridiculously large textbooks.

"All of them?" the girl asked, her brown eyes wide.

"Yep," Todd said, digging in his pocket for the receipt.

"But the semester, like, isn't over." She sounded tired. As if she were working *so* hard. It was obvious she didn't want to deal with this. Neither did Todd. But he had to.

"Just do it, please," he said.

The girl rolled her eyes but took the first book and turned toward her register.

"Todd?"

He glanced over to see Alexandra Rollins and Lila Fowler standing next to the magazine rack. Just what he needed. Todd checked his watch and sighed.

"Hey, guys," he said.

"You look like hell," Lila said, looking him up and down with a grimace.

"Thanks, Lila," Todd said. "Always nice to see you too."

Alex approached the counter, her eyes roaming over his stack of books. "So it's true?" she said. "You really are dropping out?"

Todd nodded as he watched the ponytail girl punch in a few numbers. After his conversation with Elizabeth, he wasn't surprised Alex knew. Girls and gossip seemed to go hand in hand. "It's true," he said wearily. He suddenly realized his shirt was still stuck to his back, and he didn't know whether it was from water or sweat.

"That is so cool!" Alex blurted out. "You must be psyched. Out there on your own. Living the good life."

"Not right now," Todd said, rolling back his

shoulders in an attempt to unstick his shirt. "I'm totally stressed, actually. I have to—"

"Whatever," Lila interrupted, pushing her fine brown hair behind her ear. "At least you don't have to deal with midterms. I swear I'm starting to get worry lines."

Todd felt his face grow hot. She was so clueless. But what could he expect? How could Lila I'm-richer-than-God Fowler even grasp the concept of working for a living?

"And finals," Alex put in. "And you get to sleep all day and hang out at a nightclub every night! For money!"

She made it sound like he was a rock star.

Todd felt his jaw start to clench and silently willed the ponytail girl to hurry it up. He couldn't handle this conversation much longer without exploding.

"Here you go," the clerk said, holding out a stack of cash. Todd took it and stuffed it in his pocket as Alex's eyes widened.

"Wow," she said. "I wish *I* could sell *my* books back."

I had to sell them so I could eat! Todd wanted to yell. But they obviously didn't get it, and they weren't going to.

"I'll see you guys around," Todd said flatly, grabbing his now empty backpack. He tore through the bookstore and out onto the street without looking back. He knew he wouldn't be seeing Alex and Lila anytime soon, though—because he was never going to set foot on this snob-filled campus again.

"So, you sure you want to come in for a little while?" Josh asked Nina as they hovered outside his dorm room on Saturday night.

"Of course!" Nina said with a smile. "I wouldn't have come back here if I didn't." She was having such an amazing time with Josh, she just didn't want the night to end. All he'd done throughout their entire date was prove over and over again how very not Xavier he was, and Nina was enjoying every second of it.

Josh popped open the door and checked inside. "My roommate went away for the weekend," he said, stepping aside so she could walk in first. Another very un-Xavier thing to do.

"Thanks." Nina strolled in and took off her jacket, hanging it on the back of one of the desk chairs. She immediately did the first thing she always did the first time she was in anyone's room—started checking out the pictures on his bulletin board.

"Oh God! Don't look at those," Josh said, tossing his keys on his desk and taking off his own jacket.

"This one's cute!" Nina said, pointing out his prom picture. Josh walked up behind her and put his hands on her shoulders, casually squeezing them once.

"I was such a dork," he said. "Hard to believe that was only two years ago."

Nina laughed, and then she suddenly felt something warm and moist against her neck. Josh was kissing her. Her heart immediately started to flutter at the intimacy of the contact, but the rest of her froze up. Wasn't it a little soon? Didn't most people start with a quick kiss on the lips?

Turning to face him, Nina looked into his warm blue eyes. He reached up and gently placed his hands on either side of her face, his eyes searching hers. "Is this okay?" he asked, his voice slightly husky.

It sent chills down her spine.

The question was so sweet and innocent, and the look in his eyes was so vulnerable. Nina closed her eyes, leaned forward, and kissed him lightly on the mouth. "Let's just take it slow, okay?" she said quietly.

"Sure," Josh said, backing up a little. Nina smiled at his awkwardness. Another non-Xavier point. Xavier was so smooth and, when she looked back, so calculated. There was nothing insincere about Josh. Nina could tell that what she saw was what she was going to get.

"So, if you're really interested in seeing embarrassing pictures of me, check this out," Josh said, pulling what appeared to be a high-school yearbook out from the shelf above his desk. He sat down on his bed and opened to the center of the book.

"Wow. If you're willing to whip out the yearbook, you must really like me," Nina joked as she sat down on his bed. She plopped down next to him and peeked over his shoulder.

"Not everyone is granted admission to this tome of embarrassment," Josh said with a smile. He pointed out a picture of a younger, more pimply Josh, whose eyes were half closed as he grinned out from the page.

"Aw!" Nina said, nudging him with her shoulder. "You *were* a dork."

"Very funny," he said, nudging her back as he slammed the book shut.

Nina shoved his arm with her hand, and he shoved her back. Josh tossed the yearbook on the floor with a clunk as they started to tussle. Laughing loudly, Nina attempted to get control of Josh's hands by grabbing his wrists, but he was too quick, and he grabbed hers first. Nina screamed through her laughter as he held her arms out at her sides.

"You give?" Josh asked with a grin.

Nina's heart was pounding a mile a minute as she looked him in the eye. "Yeah. I give," she said seriously.

There was a question in Josh's expression that

Nina suddenly felt the need to answer. As he loosened his grip on her, she slipped her arms around his back and kissed his neck, then his cheek, then his lips.

"Slow?" Josh asked quietly.

"Yeah," Nina said.

And then he kissed her. It was a sweet, lingering, lovely kiss that left Nina's toes tingling. Before she knew it, she was kissing him back, holding him tightly. Suddenly she felt his fingers unbuttoning her cardigan, and every nerve in her body pounded with anticipation.

So much for slow.

Nina didn't want to stop. But part of her told her she should. How was she supposed to know for sure whether Josh was as un-Xavier as he appeared to be? How could she figure this out before she got burned—again?

"Cathy!" Todd yelled over the din of Frankie's Saturday-night crowd. He rushed over to her, gripping the clipboard that held next week's schedule. "Cathy!" he shouted again when she didn't turn away from the conversation she was having with Daria, the bartender on duty.

Finally Todd had to tap her on the back. When she turned around, she was laughing, but when she saw what he was holding, her face fell.

"What's the matter?" she asked nervously.

"Did you give Monica Sunday night off?" Todd asked, clutching the clipboard.

"Yeah, why?" Cathy asked, wrinkling her brow.

Todd tossed the clipboard on the counter in frustration. "Because Annie already had the night off and now the two of them are in the back room screaming and crying. One of them has a date, and the other one has a wedding to go to."

"Oh God," Cathy said, putting her hand over her heart. "I feel so bad. What do we do?"

Somewhere in the bar a glass crashed, and a few people applauded. Todd felt like someone had just broken it over his head. He was so tense, his skin was crawling.

"You're gonna have to fix it," Todd said. Suddenly a couple of guys started yelling somewhere across the bar, and Todd tried to ignore it and focus on the task at hand. "Talk to them after the shift." He looked around and then leaned forward, talking directly into her ear. "And stop letting Daria hand out free drinks to her friends," he hissed, glancing up at the bartender as she comped one of many beers that night.

"What?" Cathy said. "I didn't—"

"Save it, Cathy," Todd spat, the words coming out harsher than he'd intended. He sighed and tried to tone it down. "I saw you *ignoring* her when she gave those guys four long necks before. If Rita finds out, she's gonna fire you both."

"Fine," Cathy said, her eyes hardening even though she looked as overwrought as Todd felt.

"Okay, can you go tell Ryan it's time for his break?" Todd asked. At least that was an easy job. Cathy had to be able to handle it.

"Sure," Cathy said with a tight smile. "I'll be right back." She disappeared into the crowd, and Todd gave himself a moment to breathe. Rita wasn't kidding. Cathy was a total wash. Since they'd been here, or since Cathy had arrived late as usual, all she'd done was hang out behind the counter while Todd did all the work—cleaning up messes, cashing out registers, and cutting people off. He was about ready to drop, and it seemed like Cathy hadn't lifted a finger all night.

Another round of shouting broke out, this one louder than the last, and Todd snapped to attention when he heard a quick scream. He immediately dove into the crowd, elbowing his way over to the dartboard, where the noise seemed to be coming from.

The crowd was backing away from a couple of thirty-something guys who had grabbed each other by their shirts and looked ready to hit the floor, punching. Todd looked around for the source of the scream and saw Cathy standing by the wall, crying.

It was all Todd could do to keep from sighing in exasperation. He had more important things to deal with.

"Break it up, you guys," he said, stepping up to the men, who had started to circle around in a scuffle. Todd knew from experience that men this sloshed could barely stay on their feet, let alone throw a decent punch. It took him a couple of minutes, but he separated them and managed to get them outside.

"Call them a couple of cabs," he told Daria when he got back inside. He fell onto a bar stool and took a deep breath, trying to calm himself down. Only a few more hours and this night would be over.

Suddenly a pair of arms were flung around his neck, and Todd looked down to find Cathy pressing her face into his T-shirt, crying. "I can't do this, Todd," she said. "I really don't want this job."

Todd couldn't believe it. How could she be so stressed out when she hadn't even worked all night? Of course, he didn't say that. He just patted her on the back and waited for her to calm down.

Finally her tears subsided, and Cathy looked up at him sorrowfully. "I'd much rather be the bartender and stay back there where I'm safe instead of dealing with all this hell," she said.

Thank God! Todd thought.

"It's okay, Cathy," he said, giving her a hug. "I'm sure Rita will understand." *Especially since she knew this was going to happen,* he added silently. Relief washed through him as Cathy disentangled herself and went back behind the bar. This job would be much easier to handle without Cathy messing it up every five seconds. He liked the girl, but she was one sucky manager.

It seemed he really did deserve this position after all.

Sam put his head down on the pillow at the end of Floyd's living-room couch and heard a loud crackle. He reached underneath the tattered cushion and pulled out a half-eaten bag of stale Cheez Doodles.

"You have to be kidding me," he said, crumbling the bag up in his hand. He swung his legs over and got up, padding into the kitchen. His bare feet stuck to the cold linoleum, making a little tearing sound every time he stepped. Sam grimaced. If his housemates thought *he* was bad, they should check out this place. In fact, he thought he might take them for a little tour someday just so they could see how bad they *could* have had it.

Sam opened the cabinet under the sink and tossed the bag onto the mound overflowing from a cracked plastic trash can.

"Not my problem," he muttered to himself. He just hoped he didn't find any more tasty treats in his temporary bed. He wasn't sure if he could deal with finding a banana or a cupcake or something.

Chuckling, Sam made his way back into the living room, stepping lightly just in case his foot found a Nintendo game pad or a Monopoly hotel or something. Elizabeth, Jessica, and Neil would freak out if they ever saw this place. They'd probably all run in the opposite direction.

He plopped down on the couch once more and stretched out, his mind immediately turning to Elizabeth. Once he'd conjured up an image of her, his brain couldn't let her go. It was like he was brainwashed or drugged.

What was she doing right now? What was she thinking? A cold, hard emptiness opened up in Sam's chest as he thought about how much she must hate him right now. She was an intelligent girl. It was one of the things he liked best about her. But it also meant she was smart enough to have realized by now that he was avoiding her.

Sam rolled over onto his side and squeezed his eyes shut, trying to squeeze out the images of Elizabeth, disappointed, hurt, maybe even crying. He'd wanted to kill Finn when he'd made her feel that way. And now he was probably making her feel that way himself.

What kind of person was he?

"That's it," Sam told the empty room, bringing his fists to his temples. He had to get Elizabeth Wakefield out of his mind before he went crazy. Before he did something stupid.

Todd sank into a chair in the back room as Monica, Annie, Daria, Ryan, and Cathy finished cleaning up out on the floor. Rita slid his paycheck across the table to him, but Todd could barely lift his arm to pick it up.

"You might want to look at that," Rita said, amused. "It reflects your new salary."

With all the effort he could muster out of his weary body, Todd pulled the envelope toward him and tore it open. He was pleased to see it was actually more than he thought it was going to be, but he couldn't even get his mouth to form a smile. All he wanted right now was his bed.

"Thanks," he said, managing to fold the check into his back pocket. He folded his arms on the table and dropped his head onto them. "Tired," he blurted out.

He heard Rita laugh and shift in her seat. "So I looked at your marketing paper," she said slowly.

That got Todd's attention. He lifted his head and rested his chin on his forearms.

"And?" he asked warily, noting her not-so-psyched expression.

"You've got some good ideas, Todd," she said, running a hand over her mane of curls, "but they're not realistic. You have to think of the clientele and what this place can actually handle when it comes to special events." She laughed and looked at him fondly. "This isn't an arena, you know. Mud wrestling is out of the question."

Todd's heart felt heavy, but he let out a wry

laugh. After all, he needed to hear stuff like this if he ever wanted to grow up and stop being the idealistic college kid. This was the real world—the world he'd wanted to experience. And Rita was giving him a big helping of reality right now.

"Why don't you go home?" Rita suggested, standing up. "You look like hell."

"You know, you're the second person who told me that today," Todd said, pulling himself out of the chair. Unfortunately the last thing he wanted to do was go outside. It had started raining again, and Todd really didn't relish the idea of walking all the way home.

At that moment Ryan burst through the doors and lifted his chin in Todd's direction. "You want a ride? Since it was raining, I took the car, not the motorcycle."

Todd almost cried out of gratitude. "You're talking to me now?" he asked, picking up his jacket.

Ryan grinned. "I got over my attitude when Cathy told me what you did for her," he said, clapping Todd on the back. "Besides, I figure us working stiffs gotta stick together."

"Thanks," Todd said as they made their way through the now quiet bar. "But this doesn't mean I'm going to cut you any breaks."

"I figured that," Ryan said. They called out good-byes to everyone as they headed outside. Then they both ran for the car before they could get soaked through. Ryan quickly unlocked the driver's-side door and flipped the automatic lock. Todd practically fell into the car.

"So, listen," Ryan said as he started the engine and checked the mirrors. "I'll keep driving you if you need me to, but you've gotta get yourself some wheels, man."

"I know," Todd replied, shaking his head as Ryan swung out into the street. "I don't know what I'm gonna do about that."

Ryan patted the dashboard of his Mustang and looked at Todd. "Well, I got this baby at a really cool used lot downtown," he said. "I'm sure they could cut you a deal."

"Yeah?" Todd asked, checking out the interior of the car. The seats creaked like they were new, and the upholstery was almost spotless. Todd would have never guessed Ryan had bought it used.

"I'll take you down there tomorrow if you want," Ryan said, casting him a sidelong glance. "That is, if you don't mind fraternizing with the lowly help."

Todd smirked. "I think I can handle it."

Ryan laughed as Todd pulled out his paycheck and scanned it again. He was going to be making good money in no time. And if he could budget himself, he could definitely afford payments on a used car. And it *was* a car he should buy—not a Harley-Davidson, which was what he really wanted. A car was more practical. More grown-up.

With a long, relaxed sigh Todd leaned back in his seat and closed his eyes, enjoying the ride.

This was the first night of the rest of his life.

Check out the **all-new**....

..... Sweet Valley Web site—

www.sweetvalley.com

New Features

Cool Prizes

The **ONLY** official **Web site!**

Hot Links

.... And much more!

Bantam
Bantam Doubleday Dell

BFYR 202

You'll always remember your first love.

Love Stories

Looking for signs he's ready to fall in love?

Want the guy's point of view?

Then you should check out *Love Stories*. Romantic stories that tell it like it is—why he doesn't call, how to ask him out, when to say good-bye.

Love Stories

Available wherever books are sold.

www.randomhouse.com

BFYR 209